I0518312

MIRROR OF A STAR

a novel by

SHELDON R. SMITH

Publications

This book is a work of fiction. All names, characters, places, or events are creations of the author's imagination and are used in a fictional way. Any similarity to actual scenarios, events, locations, persons, living or dead, is totally coincidental. All poetry lyrics used throughout this book belong to the author. Copyright © 2010 by Sheldon R. Smith.

Back cover photo by: Picture Perfect Photography by Mark

SRB Publications
P.O. Box 173
Kirbyville, TX 75956

First printing: July 2010

Don't judge a book by the cover
Neither the writings of the work
After reading you may find in you
The star awaiting to be birthed

To my readers:

This book is written not to cast judgment nor to create a bad reflection on the author. It's written to use the pains and hurts to sympathize with the reader and also to ignite that superstar person inside of you so that you can turn your sorrow to success. It is my desire that after reading this book that you live out all of your dreams and become that great and awesome person you desire to be, and also that great and awesome person God desires you to be.

Mirror of a Star

Mirror of a Star

1

"OK, I can do this... ah, no I can't," I told myself as I stood in front of the dressing room mirror at the SpeakEasy Café trying to get it together for this next act.

The SpeakEasy was a local café here in Atlanta and local residents who were into jazz and a melodious atmosphere gathered here nightly. I was up next to give the poetic piece that I composed. Aside from working at Jona's Bar & Grill, I spent my nights here at the SpeakEasy.

I sort of had a thing for poetry but for some reason I wasn't a star on stage, or so I thought.

"Up next," the host said. "We have Calvin Harris."

Oh no, that's me. I was up next and not sure I even had it together. I rushed down the hallway heading to the stage. My palms were sweaty and jitter was in my every step. I approached the stage with nervousness.

I looked out over the audience as anticipation smeared their faces. I can do this, I kept telling myself. I cleared my throat and then:

"Tonight, I give you one of my most recent poetic pieces:

THE UNKNOWN

Boredom's set in like a rich stain and twenty-four hours have passed
Nothing to show worth proving to last
Anguish of a seclusion entangled to mind
An unction within to get on my grind
The ability to feel, will, and act is pain
Forever in a day is to forever love in the rain
With no secrets to tell no advocate to bail
A consumption as worst as rage in a cell
Touching the walls of intellect and wit, they don't react back
They enclose you tighter till delusion turns fact
Tears falling down the face, to my hand they fall as blood
A heart issue leaking the soul as water leaking a pipe does
Who to tell no confidentiality in site
Secrets grow stronger and urgency in the heart's as bold as night
So as I sit back and wonder what'll unfold next
The very thought makes my being of a total vex
The need to liberate but no one to unwind
Is as a striking blow knocking you unconscious one time
As I journey on to see what this enigma may bring
With no one, no thing, no bell may ring
A time bomb ticking, a picture not painted
On the wall of heart the stained epitaph tainted
No glosses and no flashy flosses
Heart feels about as cold as Jack Frost is
The soul and mind as dexterous waves tossin'
So as pain and experience are knitted by time
And these verses are not curses but lines that I rhyme
May soul glow and heart shine
I'll unravel myself and fall away one time"

    The audience cheered as though they really did enjoy it. I didn't see the big deal. What was music to their ears was another writing piece that bellowed from within. However, I did do better than I thought I would have.

    I went into the dressing room and gathered my stuff to leave. I wasn't the type to hang around to find out the verdict. Besides, it was late and it was a surprise that I stayed out this long.

I guess I shouldn't be so surprised seeing how I was out late mostly every night doing my poetry here at the SpeakEasy.

It was late spring and the air was slightly humid as I stood out in front of the SpeakEasy allowing the humidity to saturate my face. The damp night air filled the streets as cars passing by splashed water puddles in the road.

It was closing time as the regulars of the café headed to their vehicles. I should be leaving as well but I decided to stand there and savor the moment even though it was after one in the morning and I had to be at Jona's bright and early for 8:00.

"Oh, I loved that poetry piece, Calvin," Mrs. O'Hara said, leaving out of the front door. She and her husband were regulars here.

"Yeah, Calvin you really got a heart for poetry," Mr. O'Hara added.

Mr. and Mrs. O'Hara were good people. Every time they spoke to me I knew they were going to say something encouraging. That's one thing I enjoyed about Mrs. O'Hara when I was in her presence—she was always encouraging. She reminded me of a distant aunt who would try to lift your spirit and build you up whenever she saw you. I decided to head on home.

I walked over to my '98 Toyota Camry. Man, I love that car. Some nights I would just hop in and hit the streets. The city life at night was pleasant and peaceful here in Atlanta. I enjoyed viewing the well-lit buildings and riding through the night air with my window down allowing the wind to hit me in the face. The people were always moving from one hot spot to the next, looking for hedonistic fun and pleasures. It was a busy city at night and yet it was so peaceful as well.

I headed back across town to the Shade Ville apartments where I stayed. The rent was high but I managed to get it paid on time. There were a few times where I would lapse in payment trying to pay other bills.

My car was a present from my uncle when I graduated high school back in 2000. My parents moved to North Carolina after graduation and I stayed here in Atlanta. I graduated college with a Bachelor's in Business Management back in 2004. Now I'm 26 and it's kind of my dream to own Jona's Bar & Grill one day. Jona says that if I work harder, in a few years I'd be fit to own the place. If I work harder.

I opened my apartment door and tossed the keys on the dresser locking the door behind me. Sometimes you'd have to be careful here at Shade Ville because every now and then someone would try to break in your apartment and mug you.

I took off my coat and hung it in the closet. The smell of pizza had a light scent in the air from earlier. I turned on the T.V. but there wasn't much on. I laid across the bed looking at the T.V. until my eyes grew heavy. Next thing I remember I drifted off into a peaceful sleep.

2

Buzz! My alarm went off. Oh no, 8:15—I'm going to be late. I hoped that Jona wouldn't bite my head off but it wouldn't be the first time and definitely not the last. I had to shower and get the heck out of here.

Ah, the water felt good splashing against my face. I was going to need refreshment before facing the day because Jona's could get pretty hectic at times. I hurried, dressed and grabbed a Pop-Tart off the counter. I rushed downstairs and out to the car and by this time it was 8:32—I knew I had it coming.

I pulled up into the parking lot as fast as I could. Tony was looking at me out the window. I could hear him now picking fun and telling jokes. He was my best friend. He and his family were Hispanic and when Tony moved here to Atlanta he started working here at Jona's. For some reason we meshed well together as friends.

I rushed in the door and to the kitchen. I could smell the smoking aroma of charbroiled steaks mixed with grilled onions filling the kitchen. There were busybodies everywhere. It was an assembly line—as I called it—formed at the counter preparing mashed potatoes, green beans, carrots and other delectable choices to choose from.

Dan was taking several of the produce boxes outdoors for disposal. I hurried to tie my apron

"Calvin Harris, do you know what time it is?" I turned around and it was Jona.

Jona was a middle aged short, heavy-set black woman. Her hair was short and she would wear the ends flipped out. Her facial expression was one of glee and solicitude.

"Yeah, Jone I'm late," I responded tiresomely.

"Calvin, how many times am I gonna have to get on to you about being late."

"I'm sorry, Jona I'll do better next time."

"Huh, next time," Jona startled. "How do you know it will be a next time?"

Jona always rambled off to me with her motherly tone and persona. She'd always say that and next time she would always let me slide by. I was one of her best workers—how could she resist.

"What up, Cal," Tony said to me as I walked out into the dining hall.

"Nothin' much. What about you?"

"Aw, you know me, my brakes always on chill."

Tony had a way with words. He was one of those cool cats with slick black hair and Latino features. He was my boy and I enjoyed hanging out with him—sometimes.

"So, listen man, I'ma head over to the Black Gazon tomorrow night... wanna hang out?"

The Black Gazon was a new sedative joint just built up in downtown Atlanta. It was setup as a mellowed club where cool cats like Tony and other mellowed out people would meet up.

"I can't, Tony... I got a gig at the SpeakEasy tomorrow night." I tried to shun away from the idea. Tony would probably get me caught up in some of his shenanigans.

"Cool. So, since you gotta a gig tomorrow," Tony persisted, "why don't you do it early and we head over to the Gazon afterwards."

The offer sounded tempting but I couldn't afford it.

"Nah, I gotta get my stuff together for tomorrow night." Another lie and boy did he hate it.

Tony was my best friend but I had to stay focused on my dream, well at least another one of them. Going to the Black Gazon would've been good but I couldn't jeopardize my poetic skills.

Plus, I knew the Black Gazon would be full of luscious beauties prowling and looking for a young soul like myself, though. The thought of attention was tempting.

"C'mon man, you know it's gonna be some hottie there you can push up on," Tony persuaded.

He was right. There probably would be some hot chick there for me to "scoop up". Lord knows I needed a woman—or so I thought.

"Maybe some other time, Tone."

"Well… alright, I guess I'll let you make it this time." He turned and went back to what he was doing.

Maybe I should've said yeah instead. My life was humdrum outside of poetry at the SpeakEasy and Jona's Bar & Grill. I hadn't had a girlfriend in three years and the last girl I was with was a sham that should've never happened.

Tamica Robbins—the worst relationship of my life. Oh, gosh! Tamica was a 5'9 mocha-skinned woman. She was very attractive but anyone who had eyes could see she was seductive. I don't mean seductive as in wooing you with her eyes but it was a seduction as in, "I got you and a couple other men's noses wide open", so to speak.

After going with her for about a month I started noticing other men picking up on her trail. Every time I would try to spend time with her she was never available and she expected me to follow her—please. When I caught wind of her so-called "associates" I cut her loose.

"Calvin, when you get done bussing tables take out the trash," Jona shouted from the kitchen.

"Ok," I replied. I had to stay on top of things because Jona wasn't going to give me a break. Sometimes she was always on my case but—it would keep me in line.

My shift ended at 4:00 and boy was I tired. Today was pretty busy and I did well in collecting tips.

"Let's do it again tomorrow," Tawny said sarcastically as I was getting into my car.

Tawny was a young brown-skinned woman. She was light-hearted but you could see the despondency in her dark brown eyes and she was pretty far spent in disconsolation.

"Same place, same time," I replied.

I cranked up and hit the highway to get a handle on the five o' clock traffic that awaited me.

I turned to 98.5 on my radio. Doug Madigan was on. Doug, or DJ Doug as he was well known as, reviewed some of the highlights of the day. It was the usual: the battle against hip-hop in society, celebrity marriages and breakups, athlete incrimination, and so forth. After fifteen minutes of listening to society's problems I turned it off—I had problems of my own.

I took a short cut off the highway to get to Shade Ville quicker. Luckily, I was able to make the shortcut today. Other days I had to battle road-raged drivers or someone standing on the side of the road trying to sell some type of food or health care product.

In the parking lot of the apartments, everything looked peaceful—for now. There were no arguing neighbors or youngsters in the parking lot drinking, smoking, and talking about know-nothings.

As I walked up the stairs to my room, I could smell Betty frying chicken as usual. Betty stayed a floor below mine. Every time I went up the stairs to my room I would get a whiff of her home cooking on the way up. Sometimes I wished that I could take some of her food to my room.

I laid my things down and tried to unwind somewhat. I checked my messages on the answering machine:

"Yo Cal, this ya boy. Just checkin' to see if you were still up for tomorrow. Now I know you said you couldn't go to the Black tonight but I thought I'd try you out to see if you changed your mind. Holla at me when you get this."

I already told Tony that I couldn't go to the Gazon tomorrow. It was a tempting offer but I had a gig tomorrow night.

He just didn't get it. Next message:

"Hey Calvin, this is Erica. I know you probably heard about the Black Gazon opening tomorrow night. Me and Aliyah were gonna go and check it out, so we thought you and a friend might would wanna join us. Call me back at 555-3847. Talk to ya later. Bye."

Wow! Erica and Aliyah actually called me to hangout— that's a shocker. I had to call Tony so we could double date. I just got on his case and now I needed him.

Aliyah and Erica were two young women I met at the photocopy center a week or so ago. I had to get some copies made so while I was there I met Erica and made small talk. Erica was pretty cool. I didn't know about Aliyah that much but I guessed that she was a cool person herself.

I had one message left but I was so excited about the date that I didn't check it. I called Tony up and told him the news.

"Yeah, man, so she called and wanted to double date," I explained.

Tony carried on with excitement. "Aw, man, now that's what I'm talkin' about. Yo, you never know what might pop off."

I had to try to settle Tony back down because at some point in our conversations he had to always go to the left. "Yeah, Tony… let's just go out, have a good time and make the best of it, alright."

"Alright, man whatever," he said. "Look, I'll get at you tomorrow." We both hung up after that.

I decided to call Erica back to set up a time to meet. We arranged a time so now the date was set. Who knows, this could be a chance to meet the girl of my dreams.

3

I left the house about 6:45 the next evening. I had called Jeff at the SpeakEasy and told him that I couldn't make it tonight—I had other things to do. Hopefully I wouldn't let him down too much.

I swarmed myself in the scent of Calvin Klein's *Obsession Night* cologne in hopes that it wouldn't cause an obsession. I wore black slacks and a black button down shirt with a violet-colored blazer. I wasn't a flashy dresser but dark colors blended well with my brown skin and wavy hair. The colognes I wore brought out the mystic of my personality—or so I thought.

I pulled up in Tony's driveway to pick him up. He was dressed cool as usual in his dark denim jeans, black button down, and mustard-brown corduroy blazer. That was Tony—cool as ever.

" I can't believe you changed your mind," he said as we were riding along. "What about the gig at the café tonight?"

"I called and told them that I wouldn't be there tonight… I had other plans." We both laughed out loud as we rode off in the Atlanta night air.

The night was vibrant and the city was well lit, as always. It was slightly cool that night with a gentle breeze blowing every now and then.

"So you think we got it made with these girls, man," Tony asked.

"Who knows, the night's still young."

I pulled up at the entrance of the Black Gazon. There was valet parking—classy. The parking attendants wore red blazers with the lapels trimmed in black, crispy white button down shirts and black bow ties and slacks.

Everything was prompt, neat, and fashioned orderly. I stepped out of the car and handed the attendant my keys.

"And here's your ticket, sir," he said handing me the ticket. He was extra friendly with his curly black hair, dark eyes, fair skin, and thin white smile. He'd put you in the mind of a bellboy in an upscale hotel.

Tony and I stood in line waiting for the doors to open.

"You see 'em," he asked.

I looked around trying to search for them. "Nah, I don't. Maybe we'll meet up with them inside."

We looked around at all the people that showed up for tonight's festivities. The line was so long as all colors of people waited in anticipation. The Black Gazon was elegant. The building front was dull black with asphalt texturing. The sign **THE BLACK GAZON** was designed in neon green lights at the building's top.

The walls on both sides formed a triangular shaped foyer leading to two golden double doors—it was a masterpiece. The foyer was trimmed in white lights that flickered systematically giving the front building a jubilant look.

The two doors opened and a man in a black tuxedo exited.

"Good evening ladies and gentlemen, welcome to the Black Gazon." He looked like a ring announcer for a boxing match. "It's my pleasure to announce our grand opening and is of utmost sincerity that you enjoy yourselves."

The crowd applauded courteously.

"With that being said… let the celebration begin."

He stepped to the side as people clapped and entered hastily. This was probably going to be a night to remember.

4

The inside was very spacious. There were long chandelier lights hanging from the high-to-the-sky ceiling. The walls were burgundy and beige and black marbled tables and black cushioned chairs were spaced out orderly on the center floor. The bar's counter top was granite and the base was solid black.

Tony and I sat at a table in anticipation of our guests. I sat at the table searching to see if I could see Erica and her friend but I didn't see them anywhere.

"Hey man, why don't you call 'em up," Tony said eagerly.

I reached in my pocket for my cell. Now what was the number, I thought to myself. Before I could dial…

"Hi fellas," a sweet voice said to us. I looked up and there they were.

"Hi ladies," Tony and I said simultaneously.

They were so beautiful. Erica was wearing a gold, silk dress that came just above her knees. The silk material looked soft and delicate almost as if it were imported. Her stiletto heels matched the color of her dress and her soft, sheen black hair, light gold lipstick, and makeup complimented her brown skin and star-stunning attire.

Aliyah wore a sleek, black lace dress with solid black stilettos. Her silver accessories were astounding as her brown hair with light brown streaks coincided with her toffee-colored skin. Aliyah wore little makeup because she was one of natural beauty.

"Mind if we sit down," Erica asked softly.

I stood up to pull her chair out for her. Tony, in a daze, scrambled to assist Aliyah.

"So, you ladies thirsty," Tony asked charmingly. I wasn't sure if that was the right first time response.

"Sure," Erica replied. She looked timid but underneath you could tell that she was one of extraordinary potential.

Tony snapped for a waiter. A tall gentleman in a white shirt tucked in black slacks with a velvet vest came to assist us.

"Yeah, could we get four margaritas? That's cool for everybody, huh?" Tony in ways talked as if he had no elegancy but that was his character.

We all nodded in agreement. Margaritas—I didn't need too many of them. I had to be at work in the morning. I don't think Jona would appreciate me coming into her spot with a hangover trying to wait tables.

We all sat in silence for a moment. I could hear the tension in everyone's mind… I was sort of tense myself.

"So, ladies, did y'all have a pretty good day," Tony asked breaking the ice.

"Pretty good," Erica replied bashfully. I was curious to meet that other person underneath the shyness.

"How's business down at the photo shop," I asked looking at Erica. I felt sort of dumb for asking but really we all were asking some pretty shallow questions.

"Business has been pretty steady," Aliyah responded. The question was intended for Erica but Aliyah took a shot at it.

There was something mysterious about Aliyah, almost like some kind of enigmatic seduction. Whatever the case, I had to be careful. The waiter returned with our drinks. Four margaritas in a martini glass—how nice.

I wasn't fond of drinking but to be a socialite I decided to blend in. I couldn't let the girls see my innocence. As for Tony, on the other hand, I didn't care if he did. There were many things he'd try to persuade me to do and I'd leave him on a limb by himself as usual.

I took a sip of the margarita. There was a burning sensation to it; I could tell I wasn't a drinker. Tony, however could down more alcohol than anyone I knew. Maybe that's what he did back in Mexico… I don't know.

"So, you fellas feel up to dancing," Aliyah asked with a look of spontaneity in her eyes.

I wasn't a dancer—by any means. The last time I danced was senior prom and that was because someone spiked the punch.

"I'm down," Tony replied.

"What about you Calvin," Aliyah asked looking at me mystified.

I tried to shun the idea. "I'm not sure if…"

"C'mon, Cal it'll be fun," Erica interjected.

Well, if "she" insists then I guess I could attempt to bust a few moves. I could see the bitter expression on Aliyah's face. I really was the one she intended to dance with. I followed Erica to the dance floor while Tony pushed up on Aliyah. I don't think she liked that.

There was a reggae song playing but I wasn't sure which song it was. I danced to the best of my ability—what little I had. It was fun. The atmosphere was filled with eminence and harmony as everyone had fun together and yet individually according to their own personal style and elegance.

The Gazon closed down at two. Everyone gathered outside to say their goodbyes and adjourn to their vehicles. It was partly cloudy as the moon revealed its shining light behind the scattered clouds.

"Well, I guess we'd better get goin'," Erica said.

I hate that I didn't get a chance to get as acquainted with her as I would've liked to, but another day and another time.

"OK. Would you like me to walk you to your car," I asked politely.

"Sure that'd be nice," Erica replied with a smile.

We walked and talked as Tony and Aliyah were walking a few feet behind. I don't think Aliyah was really into Tony. I don't know why, he was a pretty cool fella.

"So, you got another busy day at Jona's huh," Erica asked.

"Yeah, that's probably the plan." I tried to play it cool with her, being that it was my first impression. I couldn't afford to mess up.

"I'm sure glad that I didn't drink too much," I said. "That would've been really messed up." We both laughed.

Erica was so beautiful to me. I think it was her modesty that I found attractive. She was so calm and yet amusing.

We arrived at her 2004 Lincoln LS, silver—nice. I opened the door for her. I could feel the jealousy coming from Aliyah and burning away at the back of my neck like a cigarette lighter.

"Thanks," Erica said as she was seated inside. "And thank you for a wonderful evening." I tried to keep from blushing.

Tony opened the door for Aliyah and as she got in he closed the door for her. As the two drove away Tony and I went to the car. When we were inside Tony asked questions and chattered away.

"So what did you think, bro," he asked.

"She's nice," I replied passively. "Really nice."

"You think you'll score with her?"

"C'mon, Tone… it's more to women than scoring." Tony's mind was on sex but it was more to Erica than sex. I wanted relationship and friendship and love.

Tony continued to talk and carry on but my mind was on Erica so I sort of tuned him out. I dropped him off at his house and floated off into the night air.

I opened the door to my apartment. Things were fairly quiet tonight, no arguing couples, no partying out in the parking lot… just quietness. I looked in the fridge for something to snack on. There wasn't much to choose from. Man, I needed to go grocery shopping.

I made a bologna sandwich and drank a small carton of fruit punch. Once I finished with it I prepared my clothes for the next day. The time started getting away from me and the night grew later.

I lied down at almost three-thirty. I had to prepare myself for another busy day at Jona's tomorrow. My cell phone rang as I was lying there. Who could this be?

"Hello?"

"Hi, Calvin," a soft voice said.

It was Erica, I thought to myself. "Hey, what's up, Erica?"

"You're up. I just wanted to call and holla at cha since we didn't get to talk tonight," she said

I did talk to her, what was she talking about? "What do you mean?"

"I mean you kinda pushed me off on your friend and I didn't really get to spend time getting to know you."

This must have been Aliyah. "Spend time," I asked. "What do you mean spend time?"

"You know, see if me and you had something goin'. I saw you talkin' with Erica but I just wanted to see if me and you had a thing together."

"A thing," I blurted out. "What kind of a thing are you lookin' for?" I tried to stay on the lighter side of things—I didn't want to ruin my chances with Erica. Besides, I didn't really know Aliyah and how in the world did she get my number.

"Oh, so you don't know what's up now," Aliyah said sarcastically. "You just gon' play me like you don't know what's up?"

"Actually, Aliyah, I really don't know what is up, nor what you are talkin' about. Plus, I don't think your friend, Erica would appreciate how you blockin' on the cool."

"Blockin'," Aliyah exclaimed. "I ain't blockin', baby we just talkin', and besides, I don't know why you trippin' like you really don't wanna holla."

"Aliyah, I don't know what kinda game, or whatever you wanna call it, you got goin' but I'm about to holla at you later cause I gotta get up early and I ain't got time for this."

She laughed shockingly. "I can't believe it. You're serious, huh?"

"Yeah I'm serious," I replied. "I don't even really know

you and I don't know where you got the impression that me and you had a…thing, or whatever, together."

"And you hardly know Erica," she snapped back. "So where does that leave us?"

I began to grow tired of the back and forth commentary. "Aliyah, check it, I'll see you when I see you, but right now I gotta go."

She paused for a moment. "Alright, I guess we'll talk more later."

This chick was persistent. "Bye, Aliyah." I hung up the phone. She really thought that it was a her and me.

I rolled over and went to sleep. What a night.

5

The next morning I lagged around in the kitchen joking with Tony as we recapped last night's date.

"So, man what's up wit' you and Erica," Tony asked.

"What you mean, man," I replied.

"I mean are you gon' try to get wit' her or what?"

"I don't know," I said, thinking about the question. "I'ma play my cards, kinda see where we can take this. Besides, I wanna do this the right way. You know what I'm sayin', I don't wanna be rushin' up in to somethin' until I can kinda feel my way around."

Tony looked at me startled. "Did you see the body on that girl? Man, it look like you don't need too much in the way of feelin' if you know what I'm sayin'"

"Come on, Tony, it's more to women than sex," I pleaded. "Alright, let me handle this."

Tony gave me a bland look. "Alright man, handle your business." He started to walk away but turned to me again as if he had more to say. "Look I'm just sayin', you don't wanna pass that up you feel me."

"I gotcha, man," I chuckled. Tony was always trying to push me up on some girl. I wasn't all about "pushing up", so to speak. I figured I'd just play it cool and see how things would turn out.

There was one other thing I did want to talk to him about. It was something that had been on my mind since I got up this morning.

"Hey, Tone, I wanna holla at cha about Aliyah."

Tony looked at me stunned. "What's up?"

"Man, I don't know if you know it but I think ya girl Aliyah got a thing for me."

He gave me the look of offense. "What you talkin' 'bout, man?"

I looked around to see if anyone was listening. "Last night I was gettin' ready to lay down, right, and my cell phone rang. I answered it, thinkin' it was Erica, but it was Aliyah. She called tryin' to see if me and her had a thing together. I told her I didn't know what she was talkin' about because clearly she saw me talkin' to Erica. I told her I didn't get down like that, you know. I ain't tryin' to talk to her and Erica at the same time."

Tony gave me a strong disagreeable look. "Huh, so she was tryin' to get at you?"

"I guess, man but I told her I ain't got time," I said trying to smooth things over, "and clearly she saw me talkin' to Erica."

Tony looked as if he had lightened up momentarily but I could tell he wasn't really feeling that. I just wanted to be open and honest but it looked like this honesty was about to create a wedge.

"You ain't mad are you," I asked.

"Nah," he replied, looking as if he were partially telling the truth. "You said you squashed it so… we'll see how it plays out." He left it at that and we went about our daily tasks.

I thought to myself that maybe I shouldn't have said anything, but I'd rather be up front now than suffer for it later. As he said, we'll see how it plays out.

*   *   *   *

Later on that evening I put on my rose red blazer with my black button down and denim jeans. It seemed as if I were a fan of black. The red blazer was a symbolism of love… I guess.

I grabbed the keys off the table and headed out the door

when my cell phone rang.

"Hello?"

"Yo, Cal, hey man," the voice said. It was Tony.

"What is it, Tone?"

"No need gettin' snappy." From the sound of it he was intoxicated by something.

"Tone, I gotta get out of here, I got a gig tonight."

"Cool then, lemme go wit ya." I could feel the deep-seated anger arising within me. I hoped that he didn't go out and "mess" himself up because of Aliyah's mix up.

"Not tonight, Tony. Maybe some other time, I gotta go."

"Ahh, aiyt then, maybe later," he said hanging up the phone. He probably got mad but I didn't care because he was messed up anyway. I sprayed on some Calvin Klein and headed out the door.

I cruised pretty swiftly down the Atlanta streets. Frankie Beverly's *Southern Girl* played on the radio. As it played I rehearsed my poetry over and over in my mind. Maybe I could express myself freely tonight.

The SpeakEasy was crowded again tonight and there was a line of people walking through the door. The SpeakEasy was the spot. If your day was rough, trouble surrounded you, or a co-worker got under your skin the SpeakEasy Café was the place to be. It was soothing to the soul and relaxation to the mind.

I entered in through the back door. I didn't feel up to the "hellos, how are yous or it's good to see yous," so I went around back. The backstage halls were quiet and dim. I passed up a nervous man rehearsing the failing job he had just done on stage as I walked into the small backstage room where all the talents rehearsed, acted out, and persevered to recite the perfect piece. Unfortunately, I was the only one in the room—that was a good thing.

I sat down on a wooden chair that was placed in front of a large mirror bordered with light bulbs.

"Hey Cal, your on in five," Jeff said peeping in the room.

Jeffrey Nash was a clean shaved, pretty smiling, beady-eyed black man. He hosted every night and was the man for the job. His sarcastic undertone made him, in his own right, a star among many.

I pulled out my poetic piece that I had written this afternoon. I could hear the audience applauding whoever was on stage. Well, that's my cue. I quickly shoved the piece of paper in my lapel pocket and scurried towards the stage.

"And next, the SpeakEasy's own… Calvin Harris," Jeff exclaimed. The audience clapped as I entered from behind the crimson red curtain onto the stage.

I was somewhat nervous and a slight jitter passed through my stomach. The audience silenced.

"This here is a recent piece of mine.

LOVE PAINS

Sometimes I wonder why pain hurts so deep inside
Love: an element that grows stronger everyday
To love and wish the pain would go away
The wondering why an individual suffers
The knowing that God's love hovers
It hovers over me, yet and still through dark clouds and rains
To experience love and its love pains
A love so honest and so pure
Telling each other of a characteristic of its personality we'd ensure
But now you are lost
Hidden and not to be found
An advantage passed
A dream come true now is a fantasy
Sounds of gladness are now quietness in the wind
O love, O love where art thou
O love, nowhere to be found
I'd give anything to see you again
A replenishing source of you so deep within
To meet you again in your full measure
As you are in heart trueness, and not just pleasure
Dear God I've been through it before
Oh my soul and the pain it bore
Please deliver me forevermore

Going through things you can't explain
The experience of true love and its love pains"

The audience cheered and stood to their feet as usual. I bowed and exited the stage walking off to the back room to sit down and recollect on what just happened. I felt as if I had poured my soul out to a crowd of people and what others saw as exhilarating and enchanting was a truthful expression from within.

I wanted to love, and with Erica this just could be that— love. But, I didn't want any mess like I had with Tamica. I didn't want to pour myself into someone only to have it thrown in my face. I'd been through that once; I didn't need a reenactment.

I exited through the back door and out to my car, hoping that I wouldn't be flagged down by anyone. My whole purpose for coming tonight was to stand and deliver—nothing more, nothing less.

It was humid and the smell of the streets filled the air. I unlocked my car door and decided to head home. I didn't have much of a life outside of work and Tony was messed up in the head so with that, I opened the door to the Camry to ride off.

"That was a great poetry piece, Calvin," someone said from behind me. I turned around to see who it was when I noticed it was Aliyah standing there in a red wrapped dress.

"Thank you," I replied, trying to feel out where this was going.

"I didn't know you had skills like that," she continued, "… I always knew it was more to you than just a shy charm."

I sighed, not feeling like starting this again with her. "Look, Aliyah, is there a point to all of this?"

She walked closer toward me. "Why you keep blowin' me off… like you don't wanna holla at me? Can't we just talk without all the other drama?"

"I don't, Aliyah, how many times I gotta tell you," I replied, looking sarcastically at her, "but I hardly even know you and I ain't tryin' to get into no mess with you, alright I done told you where I stand."

"I'm tryin' to get to know you," she affirmed. "And that's where I stand. I'm sayin', if you would quit brushin' me off and talk to me maybe we'd get somewhere."

I looked at her puzzled. "Really… and what do you think your friend Erica would think of this if she knew I were flirting with you after having kicked it with her the other night?"

"It depends on what you call 'flirt'," she added. "I'm just sayin'… how about me and you get out of here and go somewhere and talk."

"Let me ask you somethin'," I said. "What about Tony? Alright, what about the other night with him… didn't that mean somethin'?"

Aliyah looked as if she was trying to find a way to avoid the question. "Tony's a cool guy, alright, but he's not my type. He's cool and means well and all, but you… you're different… intriguing and… I like that about you."

"Intriguing," I exclaimed. "What does that suppose to mean?"

"It means I like your vibe, your swagger. Look, why can't we just go somewhere and mingle? Do we have to keep goin' through this dialogue?"

"Aliyah, how many times I gotta tell you I ain't…" She kissed me in mid-sentence. Her kiss was passionate and strong. I was stunned and engrossed all at the same time.

I pushed her away from me. "Are you outta your mind?"

"You know you liked it," she replied seductively. "I don't know why you keep resistin'."

I looked at her with disgust. She was pretty and all but my heart was for another woman. I wasn't some playboy looking for a midnight fling. Besides, I didn't have time to be frequent her if I wanted to get to know Erica.

I walked away to jump in my car and leave but she followed after me. As I opened the door she faced me toward her, shutting the door of the car so that I couldn't get in. Standing there she pressed the weight of herself against me

"Girl, what are you doin'! I ain't got time for this Aliyah."

She caressed my face trying to settle me down to her level, and it almost worked, but I couldn't bring myself to go along with her. I wasn't about to get into any one-night stands with her.

"Calvin, baby all you have to do is relax," she assured me.

I didn't have time to relax. As a matter of fact, I was already relaxed and if I stood there any longer buying into her lingo I'd really be relaxed. I pushed her away from me.

"I ain't got time for this," I said, opening the car door and sitting inside. I cranked up the Camry and left her standing there.

I didn't have time to get caught up in her lust and deception. Plus, I just "poured my heart out" in the arena of love on stage in a room full of people. I didn't have time for any more drama. I could still feel her kiss and the euphoria of her perfume. I hurried home and fast, I didn't want to second guess myself and do something stupid.

6

It was almost noon when I pulled up at Maxine's Photo Copy Center. I opened up one of the glass double doors. Maxine's always had that new office smell. I don't know if it was all the photo work or not but it was spacious and well organized inside. When you walked through the door, to the left was a small, rectangular shaped sitting area with seven gray cushioned chairs. There was also an oval shaped black granite table with magazines of photographic supplies.

To the right were black woodened framed photos hanging on the wall with pictures of fair-skinned women posing as cover shoot models. Some were slightly curvaceous while others were petite. There was carpet on both sides of the room and from the door to the counter, the floor was linoleum and formed a "T" shape.

I walked over to the marble counter and Erica was sitting lazily behind it flipping through a magazine. Aliyah was nowhere to be found.

"Hi," I said startling Erica. She looked up at me with those timorous eyes.

"Oh, hi, Calvin. Wow… I didn't see you standing there."

I fumbled with some photo flyers on the counter. "Listen... I was wondering if I could rap to you for just a minute."

Erica thumbed over her work sitting on the desk looking as if she had forgot her whole purpose for being there. "Uh... yeah, sure... let me just get someone to cover for me."

She turned and looked at the door behind her that obviously led to the copy center.

"Uh, Jill," she called out. Jill came walking fast out of the back.

Jill had that ingenious secretary persona. She wore her reddish-blond hair wrapped in a bun that matched her reddish-brown framed glasses. She had green eyes, tanned skin, and gave the expression of one who took pride in their work.

She walked hastily over to Erica's desk in her lavender silk blouse, black skirt and high heels.

"I need to run and take care of something," Erica whispered to her. "You mind covering for me?"

"Sure, go 'head, girl." Jill looked like an honest and sincere friend. Erica closed her magazine and walked out from behind her desk.

We stepped outside for a minute and kind of walked around a little in the parking lot.

"So what's up, Cal," she asked smiling.

I gathered my thoughts as to how I was going to answer her. She was someone I was interested in and I didn't want to mess this up.

"How's it been goin'?" I was still somewhat shaken because I didn't know if Aliyah had talked to her or what. "I know I hadn't talked to you since the other night, so I just came by to see how you been."

"Good," she replied hesitantly. "It'll be even better when I get out of here."

"Oh, you got plans for later," I teased.

She chuckled. "I might, I might. Nah, I just want to get out of here. You know, and go somewhere and have some fun."

"What kinda fun you lookin' for?"

"Well... go somewhere... hangout. Huh, anywhere but

here."

"Yeah, I here that," I replied. We were silent for a moment.

I guess this was as good of a time as any to say what I really came to say. I obviously wasn't making much progress with small talk.

"So, listen Erica," I said discreetly. "Have you talked to Aliyah today?"

She looked at me puzzled and surprised. "She came in for a little while but said she had to step out. Why, what's up?"

Here it goes. "Nah, I was just asking cause I didn't know if she had talked to you or not." Now I sounded foolish.

"Talked to me about what," Erica persisted still looking confused.

I frowned slightly as I looked at the ground rubbing my chin. "Well… look, Erica, I know what I'm about to say might sound crazy but I'ma just bein' upfront." I paused again. "I think ya girl Aliyah… well, I think she kinda got a thing for me."

Erica laughed. I didn't see the humor but whatever she found humorous about it, it had her in big laugh.

"Wait a minute," she said between laughs. "Aliyah? My girl Aliyah?"

"Yes, your girl Aliyah," I assured.

"And how did you come to this conclusion," she asked.

"Because she called me on the phone the same night we left the club. She talked as if it was something between us that she was looking for." I couldn't build up enough nerve to tell her about the kiss last night.

Now Erica was stunned. "So… Aliyah called you, the other night, and talked to you as if there was something between y'all?"

"Yes," I assured again.

"Calvin, maybe it wasn't like that," Erica said, looking in total disbelief.

"Well what else you call it," I asked.

Erica worked through her disbelief trying to find an answer. I couldn't blame her—Aliyah was her best friend. "Nah, sometimes Aliyah can come off as being upfront and direct sometimes, especially when we're somewhere that's exciting and new. She probably wanted to get your feel on it."

"She wanted to get her feel alright," I pointed out.

"Look, Calvin, sometimes Aliyah can be over zealous and direct at times but you just have to overlook her spontaneity."

I was running out of options. I didn't know how else to tell her that her friend Aliyah really liked me. "OK, next time you see her," I said, "ask her, and see what she has to say. Of course, she may not be as straight forward with you as she normally is, but…"

Erica looked at me sternly. "Are you trying to challenge me against my best friend? Look, Calvin, you're a great guy and all but I don't think it's that serious enough for us to be conflicting with each other."

I let it go. It was no point in trying to persist around her unbelief. "OK, well I guess I'll just call you later."

"Alright," she replied. I hugged her and she went back inside and I went to my car. I just left things as they were and trusted that Aliyah would get caught in her little game she was playing.

I went by Jumbo Jack's Burger Shack to get me something to eat. This place was Atlanta's own, known for down home handmade hamburgers. I'd stopped here pretty often when I didn't feel like cooking. I wasn't the chief of cooks but believe me—I could whip up something if I needed to.

I'd stick to the simple stuff like spaghetti with a pan of cornbread, and I'd even fry some chicken from time to time. I never freaked out over my cooking because I was the only one who ate it.

"Uh, yes I'd like to order the Jumbo triple stack," I said into the intercom. The lady took my order and I sat there waiting for my food.

I must have waited ten minutes before my food came out. I was getting restless; if I waited five more minutes I would have cancelled my order. The burger and fries sure looked good—and smelled good too.

"God is close to those of a broken heart," I said reading the paper in my hand. It was dark in the room and the wind howled fiercely outside. The only light in the room came from a light bulb that shined over my head. I had an all black suit on. Black—go figure.

"Hey baby," someone said, rubbing my shoulder from behind. I turned around to find Aliyah standing there.

"What do you want from me, girl," I exclaimed.

"Ooooh, so touchy," she teased. "Baby, you need to relax a little more and take it easy. You know, go with the flow."

What was this girl talking about? She was starting to become more trouble than what she was worth.

"So, it is true," someone said from across the room. The light shined in their direction. "Calvin how could you?" It was Erica.

"Wait, Erica," I stuttered. "You see this is exactly what I'm talkin' about. Look at her. Look at what she is doin'."

"It was him," Aliyah replied. "I don't know why he frontin' now. It was a whole different story the other night."

Erica looked down at the ground as tears slowly rolled down her cheeks.

"Erica, wait a minute I can explain," I said faintly. "This is not what it looks like, and she is lyin'."

"It's exactly what it looks like," Aliyah said. "I don't know why he makin' this all up."

There came a knock at the door as it pushed open slowly. I noticed that the hall was well lit and an older man in a white suit, with a white goatee and silver colored hair tied back into a ponytail stood in the doorjamb.

"I've been here at the door waiting for you. Why hadn't you answered," he said subserviently.

I looked puzzled trying to figure out who he was and what he meant.

"If you'd go with me I'd make you a very successful man," he said. He turned and walked on down the hall.

I took off running to the door trying to follow him. The door began to close as I cried out. "Wait, wait, WAIT!"

I received a knock on the door. I looked at the clock—6:47. I had fallen asleep watching *Friends* on television. I must have been dreaming. I walked to the door trying to shake the kinks out of my leg. I looked through the peephole to see a man in a suit standing there. I opened the door.

There was a white man in a mustard-brown suit that looked a size too small on him, with a white shirt and red tie. His black slick hair was combed to the right side of his head parting it on the left side. He smiled at me with his white teeth and beady eyes. I opened the door to find out who the man was.

"Hello… Calvin Harris," he asked smiling.

"Yeah that's me."

"I was told that I might would find you here," he continued. "My name is Dwight Johnson and I'm with Poetic Passions & Pacific. May I come in?"

Poetic Passions & Pacific, what kind of a name was that? I hadn't ever heard of that before. "Yeah, sure, come on in."

I stepped aside to let him in. I still wasn't quite sure what he was doing here and why in the heck would someone attach Pacific to the back of a poetry company. I knew it was kind of awkward to let a complete stranger in your apartment but the name of his company gave me a hint that he was into the poetry business.

"You can sit anywhere you'd like," I offered, motioning him to either the couch or the recliner.

"I know you're probably wondering what am I doing here," Dwight said smiling. "Well, an associate of mine was down at the SpeakEasy Café the other night."

"Oh, so you visit the SpeakEasy too," I interjected.

"Well from time to time whenever I'm in the area, which is rare, but the point is my associate heard your piece the other night and he came back and told me, 'Dwight, you gotta hear this kid named Calvin. He really is something to hear.' So I said to myself, I gotta hear him for myself."

Now this could have been a chance at fame or either this was a hoax. Either way someone heard my poetry, and it attracted some attention. Did he really think I had the talent or was this was a con man's game?

"So what do I gotta do," I asked. I was now fully alert and in tuned to what he had to say.

"Well next Friday, as you know, there's going to be the Power For Poet's battle at the Birmingham Auditorium. I'm sure you know all about how it's going to work, uh… first place winner receives $500; second place winner receives $250. If you are as good as my assistant says you are… we may have a spot for you down at the Pacific."

I was excited and puzzled all at the same time. "Why are you all called the Pacific?"

He laughed to himself. "Our company's out in Los Angeles. Los Angeles, Pacific—you kinda get the drift? Anyway, we're always looking for new talent and we do a lot of traveling state to state. This week we just happened to be in Atlanta and we were told that the SpeakEasy Café was a hotspot for new talent. If you can show me next Friday that you have what it takes, my company and I can set you up for a poetry tour that will put money in your pockets and get your name out there."

My interest grew. Here was a chance for me to become famous and in my heart that's what I really wanted. I knew I had a knack for writing poetry but this here was a chance to bring my knack to the big stage.

"And all I gotta do is prove to you that I got talent… whether I win or lose?"

"Ha! I hope that you're in it to win definitely," he teased, "but I just wanna hear what you're made of. After that…we'll move from there."

He arose from the couch with his thin, black briefcase. "Listen, you show up next week and prove to me that you're the star that you are and who my guy says that you are then we might be able to work something out."

I walked him to the door. "Well, Mr. Johnson I definitely will look into it."

"You do that," he smiled, looking back at me, "and maybe we have ourselves a deal."

We shook hands and he left. I closed the door behind him and slumped against it. "A chance to make some real money. I gotta get my stuff together."

7

I hurried to get dressed to go down to the SpeakEasy and do some poetry. I was sort of in the mood for it after talking to Dwight, and it inspired me so much that I composed an inspirational piece right before I went down there.

The crowd assembled as usual that night and I talked Jeff into letting go on stage. I hadn't scheduled to do one that night and Jeff wouldn't have mind letting me on.

"Up next," he announced. "Calvin Harris!"

The crowd cheered as I walked onto the stage holding my paper. I didn't have time to memorize it and sentiment it so I had to shoot straight from the hip. "Tonight's piece was inspired and given to me right before I came here.

DREAM BEYOND

It's farther than the eye can see
It burns deep in us and won't let down till the clock stops
It's imagination unlimited, desire exploding with excitement
It brings personal fulfillment
A sense of great accomplishment
It lives inside wide awake and sees no turning back
It transforms others

Builds legacies
Creates a hallmark of lifetime achievement
It's called "over the edge" to some
"Seemingly impossible" to others
It can be quenched and it has the power to be unleashed
It creates the best for you
It believes the best about you
It simplifies life, and introduces extractions the world has yet to see
It can be personalized or publicized
Either way it is what it is in every form of its being
So who or what is this mystery
I'll tell you
It's called a dream
And this reverie has the power to take you over the top
It uniquely fits and is one of the things you were born for
A dream
It moves in the forwardness to bring serenity in the nowness of life
And I say to you as it would
Dream beyond

  The audience paused as they took a moment to reflect on what was read. After, a motivating and heartfelt cheer was released. I felt the peace within of a job well done. I walked to the back and went into the dressing room. Looking into the mirror I began to think and sentiment. This was my life, in every shape, form or fashion. Whether rigidly put together or a diamond in the rough, it was still mine, and some days I enjoyed it and some days I didn't think much of it.

  After the SpeakEasy closed down I hung around and chattered with some of the patrons from inside. I felt that it was time to do something different. These people listen to my poetry night after night so the least I could do was hang around and mingle with them.

  "Calvin," Jeff said. "You're a good kid. I believe in you and no matter what… don't give up on your dream."

  I thought about Jeff's words. He was telling the truth. My dreams, in a sense, were the only thing I had left to keep me going. I mingled a little while longer and after that I decided to head home.

When I got home I sat on my couch thinking about the dream and how real and awkward it was. But what really stuck out to me was the man with the white suit. He told me if I followed him he would make me successful. Was this God's way of talking to me? I didn't know.

I picked up my Bible from the coffee table. I wasn't much of a saint and I hardly related to God, but I figured that the Bible had all the answers. Flipping through Psalms, I turned to chapter 31. My mom always taught me that if ever in trouble read the book of Psalms.

In you, O Lord, I have taken refuge; let me never be put to shame; deliver me in your righteousness. Turn your ear to me, come quickly to my rescue; be my rock of refuge, a strong fortress to save me...for the sake of your name lead and guide me. Free me from the trap that is set for me, for you are my refuge. Into your hands I commit my spirit; redeem me O Lord, the God of truth.

I closed the Bible and laid it back on the coffee table. I guess in my heart I really wanted to be free. I wanted to be free from broken relationships, free from the emotional pain and hurt that I felt deep inside. I'd always heard that God was the answer but how do I get to him? This guy David knew him like that, how could I?

I showered and went to bed. As I lay there, the dream and my reading from Psalms rolled over in my mind. I thought and thought until I got tired of thinking and I thought so much that it put me to sleep.

I arrived at Jona's bright and early the next morning. I ran into Tony stacking dishes on the shelf and decided to tell him about my experience with Dwight.

"So, yeah, man this Johnson guy is really feelin' my lyrics," I said excitedly. Tony looked at me with a meager look of jealousy in his eyes. I wasn't bragging but I guess that's the way he took it.

"My man Calvin, 'bout to hit it big. So... what's your next move?"

"We got this poetry battle next Friday at the Birmingham

Auditorium," I replied. "So I gotta get my stuff in order. I can't come out half steppin'."

"You right about that," Tony agreed.

There was a brief pause between us. "Hey, Tone," I said. "You still ain't heard from Aliyah?"

Tony gave me a nonchalant look. "Nah, I ain't heard from her. Tell you the truth, I wasn't really expectin' to."

"What you mean," I inquired.

"I mean girls like that, you might kick it wit' 'em one day and the next day they outta your life." Tony looked as if he wasn't worried about running into her again. His attitude showed indifference and lack of concern and I hoped it wasn't because of what I told him.

"Besides," he continued, "she ain't give me a number to call to check on her, so why bother?"

"Hey, Tony, you ain't got no beef wit' me about what I said about her the other day," I asked, wanting to make sure that our friendship was still all good. I decided not to tell him about the kiss because I hadn't built up enough nerve to delve into that.

"Nah, Bro," he replied. "You know what they say, it's just like water under a bridge." He said that and went about doing the last thing he was doing. I thought about it and hoped that I didn't offend him. But if he said it was water under the bridge—I left it at that.

I made my way back into the dining hall before Jona got a hold of me. The breakfast run was kind of slow but I knew by lunch it would be a different story. Today was grilled steak dipped in a homemade onion sauce—delicious.

I don't know where Jona got the recipe from; of course she never told us. I guess Jona's great grandmother passed on a wealth of recipe secrets before she died so she would never be at a loss for recipes.

"I sure will think about it, Mr. Boswell," I said refilling his lemonade glass. Mr. Boswell owned a music instrument shop and café downtown.

He was always trying to get me to either buy one of his custom made guitars or do a poetry piece at his café while the band played a tune to it. I thought about it but the SpeakEasy was my home. Besides, I wasn't familiar with any of the people at his café and I had this poetry bout to get ready for.

Our lunch run was busy as usual and it probably would pick up again around four. I was somewhat tired and ready to get back to the apartment to put some poetry together for next Friday. I had little over a week to get it together. I'd jot down a few lines here and there on my break at work. I just had to create that perfect piece.

On my break I sat down and let my ideas flow into one big piece called "Life".

Sitting watching time fly by
Roaring machinery in the wind, an overcast of the sky
Times and seasons bring about a change
Whether hot droughts or massive rains
Who are people but amicable souls from the hands of a
delicate Maker
Crafted to bring about success
Success that surpasses all mankind
Some are clutched by the hands of a malicious one
A monster who has brought a curse on all mankind
A mesmerizement filled with false images and counterfeit ways
Deceitfulness spreading abroad to the ends of the earth
But now…
Now there's life
Now there's life
Vitality filled with radiance and vivacity of joy
Life where the homeless are sheltered
Life where the widowed are fathered
Life where vexated men can find support and peace
Life where brokenhearted single mothers can find restoration
What is life
Life is but an extravagant spark glistening in the sun
Where is life
Life is in the Creator who gives life to everyone

It was fifteen minutes after four when I left. I turned on the evening radio as I prepared to tackle the evening traffic. I turned the station to 96.3, which was another one of those stations that talked about the garbage in society—seems like that was going around.

As the radio played, I thought about my life and where it was going. In general, I was just a young man trying to make his mark in the world through a big dream. I yearned to tell my story to the world through the epic stage of poetry. That's all my poetry was to me. It was a platform for me to take all my inner dispositions and transform them into written and spoken messages to help someone else.

My cell phone rang jolting me out of deep thought. I looked at the ID to see who it was. I didn't recognize the number but it looked familiar.

"Hello," I said.

"Hey, baby," someone answered.

"Erica?" I replied stunned.

"Nah, it's me, Aliyah." I should have known. If I knew it was her I wouldn't have answered it. I guess I should have taken note of her number the other night when she called.

"Aliyah, let me ask you this," I started. "What and why exactly do you keep tryin' to holla at me? What are you lookin' for, huh?" I could feel the anger starting to arise within me. "And the other night…the kiss and all, what was that all about?"

"You want the truth," she replied. "The truth is, I think deep inside, behind all that frontin' and playin' hard to get, you want what I want."

"Sex? Aliyah, if that's what you think I'm lookin' for you got me figured wrong. OK, I'ma tell you like I told someone else, it's more to a relationship than sex."

"But that's just it," she interjected. "We can't even form a relationship because you still stuck on all of this other stuff. Look, Calvin I ain't said nothin' about sex, alright I just wanna talk and hangout and form what you would like to call a relationship."

I began to get frustrated again. "OK, and again, what was the other night about," I repeated. "You know, kissin' me out of the blue. What was that about?"

"'Cause you look so good when you tryin' to be so mean,"
she teased. "Nah, for real Calvin, let's just go out and kick it for
one night. I'm not askin' for sex, I'm just askin' for goin' out."

I paused to try to weave through all the drama. "And if we
go out...to wherever, then what? If I go out wit' you then
afterwards you'll wanna go out again and again. What about that?
Or better yet, what about my friendship wit' your so called best
friend Erica?"

"We ain't gotta tell Erica," she stated frankly. "Besides,
I'm talkin' about me and you. All we doin' is goin' out to mix and
mingle that's all."

"That's cold," I replied. " How you gon' do your best friend
like that? What is it about me that got you pressin' so hard to get
close to me?"

She paused for a moment. "Because, like I told you the
other night, I like your style. When I heard your poetry the other
night I could tell from the sound of it that your life has a rather
unique side to it. I'm just tryin' to get to know you on that level—if
you'd let me."

"But before the other night at the café, what made you call
me in the middle of the night? You hadn't heard my poetry before
then?"

There went that silence again. I was beginning to wonder if
she was playing me or did she really want to go out to find out the
type of person I was.

"Calvin, how many times we gotta keep goin' over
this...let's just go out and kick out for one evening. That's all I'm
askin'."

I began to grow tired of the dialogue back and forth. "Look,
Aliyah, the next time you see me at the SpeakEasy... holla at me
afterwards, alright. Then we'll go from there."

"So we can go out afterwards," she asked persisting.

"We'll see, Aliyah. But I got a question...what you gonna
do if your girl shows up at the SpeakEasy, huh?" I decided to put a
little pressure on her and give her something to think about. "You
still gonna wanna hang out?"

"Is she suppose to be coming? Seems to me that I was

there the other night…not her." I could hear the messiness in her undertone.

"What if I invited her," I asked. "Then what you gon' do?"

"Then you'd be the one tryin' to cause a problem not me," she added. "I'm just sayin' Calvin, let's just go out and get to know each other a little bit more."

"Like I said, I'll get at you after the SpeakEasy," I affirmed.

"Now we gettin' somewhere," she said settled. "See that wasn't so hard now was it?" I didn't even comment. "Calvin, all I'm saying is… let's just hang out… for one evening."

"We'll see," I ended. We said our goodbyes and I hung up.

8

That night I decided to lounge at the Black Gazon. I needed a place to get away from familiar faces and pretty-girl affairs. I needed some ease for my mind. I sat at the table alone sipping on a club soda. I didn't care for any wine or alcohol that night.

The Waldorfs band played for us—a talented blend of horn and percussion. It was a smooth flow and everyone mingled at his or her own individual tables. The dull roar allowed my mind to keep a steady flow of ease. It was the first relaxing moment of the day.

I thought about Dwight Johnson and a chance to make some real money. I had a chance to be famous—who would've ever thought it? I knew I was talented in poetry but I never thought I was good enough to go big time. Maybe it's because I never had a person to really admire my work. Mr. Johnson did and for that I could be famous.

It was about 12:30 when I decided to head out. I left a tip on the table and made way for the door. As I got ready to exit a man walked up to me.

"Excuse me, don't I know you from somewhere," he asked.

I didn't recognize who he was.

"I'm not sure," I responded. "I don't really know where you could have met me." I was trying to figure out who he was and my face gave that expression.

He snapped as if who I was came back to his remembrance. "I know, the SpeakEasy Café, right?"

"Yeah, I do poetry there a lot," I replied.

"Yeah, I hear you from time to time. Man, you have a lot of deep stuff to say."

I froze, being caught off guard. "Uh… thanks," I commented, "it kinda comes natural to me I guess."

"Well, keep up the good work," he said, giving me a pat on the shoulder. He walked off and I walked out of the door.

As I walked to my car I thought about the mysteries and events that sort of transpired in my life. It seemed as if I was always thinking about what my life would become, the type of person I would be—things of that nature.

Maybe I should have been out having the time of my life but for some reason… I wasn't. I had a dream, a dream that would take me bigger than where I was right now. And one way or another, I was going to get it.

I woke up at 6:30 the next morning. My mind was roaming again as usual so I couldn't lie there any more. I walked into my living room and sat on the couch. The thought of friendship came to mind, as a matter of fact; it was the thought of friendship that awakened me. I wondered why the friendships I had were so bizarre. It seemed that there was a flaw somewhere in each one.

Tony was my best friend but I got mixed up with a woman who was supposedly interested in him, I thought. I wanted to get close to Erica but an unkind breech came between that—Aliyah. It was all just a big mix up and couldn't figure out why I was having a time developing solid friendships.

I picked up my Bible again on the notion of friendship and my dream from the other night. I kept thinking about the man in the white suit telling me he would make me a successful man. I took it as if maybe God was trying to tell me something, the only thing was I didn't really know God like most good Christian people knew him. I heard how good he was but I didn't really know what that meant.

I opened my Bible and found an interesting part in John chapter 15. I figured I'd try my hand at finding out what Jesus said about friendships. I had always heard Mrs. O'Hara talking about stuff that Jesus said. She would always tell me Jesus would be my friend. I didn't really know what that meant but whatever it meant it seemed good. I began my reading.

Greater love has no one than this, that he lay down his life for his friends...You are my friends if you do what I command...I no longer call you servants, because a servant does not know his master's business...Instead, I have called you friends, for everything that I learned from my Father I have made known to you...You did not choose me, but I chose you and appointed you to go and bear fruit—fruit that will last...Then the Father will give you whatever you ask in my name...This is my command: Love each other.

"You are my friend if you do what I say," I said to myself. I pondered that thought for a moment before I closed my Bible. How could I do what he said if I didn't know what he said. To me that was the whole misdirection of the matter.

I was dressed and ready to go at 7:30. I poured a cup of coffee then I headed for the door. I wasn't a big coffee drinker but every now and then I'd have some. As I ran down the hallway stairs rushing to the Camry, I could smell Betty's breakfast bacon fumigating the hall. I noticed that the air in the hallway felt damp and it was always quiet in the mornings—most of the time.

"Hey, Tawny you seen Tony," I asked, meeting Tawny exiting the kitchen.

"I hadn't saw him all morning," she replied. "Wherever he is he's gonna be late." And Tony was hardly ever late. He would even beat me to work on most days. I tried calling him but I didn't get an answer so I figured I'd try calling him after I got off.

After work I went by Maxine's to work out the differences

between Erica and me. I walked through the front door and Jill was sitting at the front desk.

"Hey, Jill, is Erica around?"

"Yeah, I think she is," Jill replied. "Let me check and see."

She walked in the back to the copy area. As she pushed the door open someone was standing there talking with Erica. It was Aliyah.

"Hey, Erica," Jill said. "This guy Calvin out here wants to talk with you." Erica gave the look of disinterest. She wrapped up what she was saying to Aliyah and came out of the copy room.

"Hey, Calvin what's up?" She sounded as if she was trying to perk up after a serious conversation with Aliyah.

"Uh, Erica, listen… is there anyway we could go somewhere and have lunch. I know it's the afternoon but—it's my treat." I figured if I took her to lunch that my coming here wouldn't look suspicious.

"I, uh… kinda get off in an hour," she replied. "So, I think it's kinda late for that."

"OK, then can we talk for a few minutes," I asked.

Erica gave me a disgruntle look. "Calvin, how about we talk later. I mean I got a hour left so I kinda need to be wrappin' stuff up here."

I wasn't about to wait an hour. I was curious about what her and Aliyah talked about and I wanted some answers.

"It'll only take a few minutes," I urged. "Please?"

She sighed and agreed to talk with me. We walked outside, again, as I tried to "be nosey".

She and I sat on the bench that was positioned toward the middle of the parking lot. There was a large cloth umbrella that hung over it to keep the sun from beaming down on you.

I turned in her direction when we were seated. "Did she tell you," I asked, deciding to cut to the chase.

Erica looked at me startled. "What are you talkin' about, Calvin?"

"Erica, you gotta believe me when I tell you, that girl has a crush on me no matter what anybody says." I was fully convinced in my mind. The conversation, the kiss, there was no other resolve to come to except the fact that this girl really liked me.

"You really aren't goin' to let this go," Erica said, astounding my audacity. As we sat there Aliyah came walking out the door towards our direction.

"Is everything alright," she asked.

"Yeah, everything's fine," I interjected with attitude.

Erica turned to Aliyah. She stood up and looked her in the eyes. "Aliyah, Calvin is convinced that you really like him. Is there somethin' I'm missin' here?"

Aliyah turned to me. "Uh, I don't know exactly what to say... I mean, I hope I haven't given off the wrong impression." Aliyah lied and she knew she was being deceptive. "I'm mean, I told Calvin that I hope we could be friends that's all."

"And what about the other night," I exclaimed. "Huh, what about the kiss? What about that?"

Erica looked alarmed. "Kiss? What kiss?"

"After my poetry gig the other night I met her outside," I explained. "She started tellin' me about how great my poetry was and how great I was, and in mid sentence... she kissed me."

Erica was shocked and in total disbelief. "Aliyah, is this true?"

Aliyah was at a loss for words. "Somewhat. OK, I did tell Calvin that he was a great poet but the kiss... I was under the impression that Calvin wanted to get to know me on a more personal level."

"You are outta yo' mind girl," I exclaimed. "Aliyah, you know good and well that I never gave you an impression that I wanted to be with you. If anything I wished you would get off of my case."

Erica gave an indistinctive look. "Look, I don't know what to believe right now. OK, I got my best friend gettin' the wrong impression and I got you convinced that she really likes you. I don't know, I don't know... look, Calvin, I gotta get back to work."

She walked back toward the building without a second thought. Aliyah looked at me under-eyed and followed.

"Hey," I called out to Aliyah. She turned and looked at me.

I walked up to her. "Next time you see me…don't bother hollerin' at me."

She looked at me confused. "What do you mean?"

"You know, the phone conversation…next time you see me at the SpeakEasy holla at me afterward?"

Her expression changed revealing her hidden plan. "Why you here tryin' to cause trouble," she asked. "You know Erica's my best friend."

I looked at her ignoring her so called sympathy. "Best friend? Guess you should've thought about best friend before you tried to play me." She stared at me angrily and turned to walk back inside

She knew she was wrong and here Erica was caught up in the mix. I didn't know how else to convince her but I pray that she will see what a cunning and conniving friend Aliyah was to her.

9

I made it back to Shady Groves three minutes after six. What a day. I couldn't believe all of the stuff that had happened. How in the world could a good deal have gone bad? I meet someone who I am interested in and what happens—someone else screws it up.

As I unlocked my door there was small card with POETIC PASSIONS & PACIFIC in the top left corner with a note taped to it. I opened it and read it as I walked in.

Mr. Harris,

Just wanted to touch base with you and let you know a couple of things. I know it's sort of early to be contacting you, but that's what we do when we meet potential clients.

I'd like to met with you down at the Starlite Coffee Shop this coming Tuesday to show you some of our brochures of the company. How's Tues. at 11 a.m.

Hope that's a good time. Until then keep moving forward.

Dwight

I threw the note on top of my dresser and headed to the answering machine to check the messages. After going through all of them, there were none from Tony. I tried calling his cell phone but I couldn't get an answer. I didn't know whether he was avoiding me or if he was in trouble. And to think, all of this was behind one person—Aliyah.

Aliyah was an attractive woman but her attraction mixed with deception made a bad combination. Now there was no telling what Erica thought of me, and on top of that—what did Tony think.

I looked through the fridge for something to snack on. I couldn't believe that Aliyah had tricked Erica into believing that I was the one who was in the wrong and she was somewhat right. It was crazy. I sat down on the couch and took out my writing pad and pen. I could feel the unfolding of poetic resolve bursting inside waiting to come out.

In ten minutes I had a poetic piece inscribed and I could feel the sign of relief as I closed my tablet. I really liked Erica but after today… who knows what might come of our relationship?

I had a gig at the SpeakEasy that night. As I entered the building everyone talked at a dull roar. You could feel the anticipation of excitement in the air. I wore an ocean blue colored blazer with a white button down shirt. I was kind of laid back and the blue and white color schemes symbolized my sedated eagerness to perform.

For some reason after chaos and a day of riff-raff, poetry always relaxed my mind. It was soothing almost like a pain-relieving drug. I went back into the little room in the back. There were two other guys standing in the corner on both sides of the room rehearsing their poetic pieces. I sat at the desk in front of the well-lighted mirror.

My countenance was sort of doleful and glum as I sat there and recollected on a few things. I unfolded the notebook paper with my lines on it.

"Cal, you're up next," Jeff said, peeping his head through the door at me. I had called Jeff and asked him could I perform. I crumpled up my paper and shoved it into my pocket.

"You alright, man," Jeff asked concerned.

I got up from the table. "Yeah…just some things I gotta get off my chest, you know."

He nodded in agreement. "Well, you know this is the place to do it." Jeff turned and walked out of the door

I walked slowly down the hallway to the stage unprepared and ready to unload. I walked on stage as the audience cheered me in as a regular. I was slightly nervous, upset and ready to give the performance of a lifetime.

"Tonight… I didn't have time to get it all together to memorize," I explained. "But I had some things on my mind and I wanted to express them." The crowd waited in expectancy.

THE FURY WITHIN

The fury within burns so deep inside
Fuel and adrenaline broiling from dichotomized concoctions
A burning felt deep within the mind
The agony of it arouses massive frustration
Remorse with a blend of anguishing pressure
Sympathy with a blend of gallant effort
And of this strange bewildering comes a fury
A fury burning between spirit and flesh
A fierceness springing from the abyss of the soul
A frenzy that has consumed minds whole way of thinking
For a passion transcending containment has set in
A villainous appetite that's outgrown mind's controllability
For when injustice isn't tamed it grows
And now a certain trepidation of its kind has taunted me
An ambition I wish not on anyone
A habitual deception that stages a baffle in mind
Of this conundrum kindles the fury within

There was a brief pause and hesitation. Suddenly, there was a raving sound of an outgripping performance. The audience cheered like I'd never heard them cheer before. I stood there feeling the impact that this poetic piece left within. I turned and walked hastily to the back and sat in the little room to try and collect myself.

What was happening to me? What was happening to
my poetry? It seemed as if the frustrations, daily agitations, and
dreamful bellows from within were being expressed the deepest
when I wrote or spoke. It felt strange.

I left the SpeakEasy felling down. My love life was a mess
and my friend Tony was out somewhere. The only good thing I
really had going for me was the shot at making it big and spreading
the fame of my poetry on a worldwide level. A shot at fame would
really make me feel afresh and revived right about now but at the
same time I thought—what's fame without relationship with close
friends.

I decided to take a ride through the city. I thought about
God and the stuff the Bible said about him. He chose me because
he wanted me as a friend, I thought, but I asked myself how. How
could I befriend God when my life was a mess at this point? I was
my own worst enemy and I was running on internal instinct and
misfortune.

My cell phone rang jolting me out of deep thought once
again. I wondered why every time I began to do that someone
would call. It was Tony.

"Hello," I said.

"Yo, what's happenin', bro," someone slurred.

"Who dis?"

"Who dis? This ya boy… Tony." He didn't sound like
himself for some reason.

"What's up, man?"

"I saw where you called me earlier. Yo, I'm out here in
College Park wit' my lady… chillin'." From the sound of it, Tony
was either high or drunk. I couldn't decipher between the two.
He'd been known to do some pretty eccentric things—I wonder
what he was into now.

"You done found you another woman," I asked.

"Aw, you know me," he stuttered. "You know how I get
down. I gotta get my women."

"Hey, man… what's up wit' you missin' work," I inquired.

There was a short pause. "Aw, man you know me… I had
to handle up on some stuff."

"What stuff?" He wasn't making much sense and I believe he was stalling.

"Look, man," Tony replied forcefully. "Sometimes you just gotta take a break for a while, you know. E'ryone need a break every once in a while."

A break from what, I thought. What was Tony talking about, or better yet where was all of this coming from? For as long as I'd known Tony he'd always been a stand up guy. Now he sounded like a man whose brain had went bad.

"Hey, Tone… I don't know what you've got yourself into, but I ain't really feelin' it right now." There was that pause again.

"I ain't askin' you to feel me, okay? I'm just sayin' that I need a break for a while."

"Look, man… and whatever you're on, I hope you ain't wildin' out because of what we talked on the other day."

"Hey, man, like I said, you gotta take a break sometimes," he said again.

I left it at that. "Alright, I guess I'll see ya when I see ya." I hung up the phone. I didn't have time for the games. I guess I'd have to ride this one out myself. True friends were hard to find these days—I had to see that. But at some point I would have to walk on my own two feet. What better time than now.

I had trouble sleeping that night. I looked at the clock— 2:57. I got up and paced my apartment floor in hope to relieve my mind. That didn't work.

I went to the fridge for a snack. There wasn't much in there. I would call someone but who? Tony was my best friend but his mind was shattered right now. I wouldn't mind hearing Erica's voice but after today's encounter she probably was still against me. I turned on the T.V. and to my surprise… nothing.

My life felt like it kept repeating itself. Outside of work and the SpeakEasy—this was it. I could have been out partying with Tony or Aliyah or Erica but where would that take me. I figured that everyone needed spark in their life, myself included but I didn't have it. Between the urge to dream and the quest to find meaningful relationships it would become frustrating. I walked over to my window and looked out at the city.

Atlanta was something to see at night. There was an array of lights and buildings far out and beyond. The night sky and stars blanketed the city. I looked down into the parking lot. There wasn't much going on except a guy and girl hugged up and two guys leaned against the car beside them. One had a 40 oz. and the other guy was smoking a cigarette.

I closed the blinds and attempted to doze off. The last thing I remembered seeing was the 4:03 on my clock.

It was Saturday and I was off from work. I decided to go by the mall and browse around to see if I could find anything interesting. I would have called Tony but his mind was elsewhere. I dressed fly and hopped in the Camry and headed to the mall.

When I got there the people began to pack the place out. It was Atlanta—what did I expect. I went inside of a couple of clothing stores to find something fresh and jazzy. I figured it was time to change my style up a little. I found several outfits that would look great on me. I picked up a few and went on from store to store.

As I left out of one store I began looking around at all of the people around me. Everyone looked carefree, excited, laid back and everything else. It was the look of happiness that I gleamed from the whole time being there. To watch and see how those who were in groups were happy to be around the people they were with. That's the type of relationship I was in pursuit of—happy ones.

Even a relationship with God, if I could ever get one, would probably be nice. Really I felt that if I worked on my relationship with others then maybe I could get to God. I walked and thought about all of this until I could feel uneasiness trying to set in. I threw all my thoughts to the wind. It was Saturday, I needed to chill and enjoy the moment.

I walked and glanced at store after store until I became hungry. In the midst of looking at the people I saw a young woman a few feet away from me. From the looks of it she favored Erica but she was walking with another guy so maybe it wasn't her. The closer I got to her, her physique really favored Erica and whomever she was walking with had her smiling and laughing.

I drew close enough to try to make out who she was. It was Erica but who was the guy? My heart fainted within me. Not someone else, I thought. Everything was going from bad to worse. I walked up to her to catch her off guard.

"Hey, Erica," I said sarcastically.

She looked at me dumbfounded and speechless. "Hi... Calvin. What are you up to?"

The heat of anger arose within me. "I was just... coming by to see what was new in the stores." A sick feeling overshadowed me. "What about you," I asked.

"Oh, doin' the same," she chuckled, thinking nothing of her being there with someone else.

There was a short pause. I figured I could have at least found out who the guy was.

"How you doin', man I'm Calvin," I said, extending my hand to shake his.

"Quincy," he replied. Erica looked as if she had forgotten her manners by not introducing me to her friend.

"So... y'all dating or what," I asked, trying to rub it in.

"Quincy is a friend of mine," Erica interjected. "It was Saturday and... well, I didn't have a lot planned and neither did he so... here we are." She chuckled again trying to shun her feeling of shame.

I sniggled. "Well... I hope y'all are having fun." I could feel sadness haunting me so I had to play it off. She still showed no remorse or guilt. I decided not to even hassle with it anymore.

I looked away trying to kill the mood. "Well, uh, I guess... I'd better let you two get goin'. It was nice meeting you, Quincy."

He nodded. I looked at Erica and could see she was convinced that this was who she wanted to be with.

"I guess I'll... see you around, Calvin," Erica added, nonchalantly.

"Yeah, I guess so." I looked at both of them and kept walking. My heart fluttered and the "fury within" took its toll on me.

I left the mall feeling sad, angry, betrayed, and depressed all at the same time. But, that's how the game went and like the saying goes: what are friends for.

10

When I made it home I tossed the keys on the dresser and plopped down on the couch. I couldn't believe it—Erica was with someone else. This was all Aliyah's fault. Because of her Erica didn't want to have anything to do with me and it was the deception of her so-called best friend. What a way to spend Saturday—seeing the woman you had feelings for in the arms and presence of another.

I was so disturbed I decided to put my frustration to the pad. I pulled out my notepad and wrote lyrics just as fast as they poured into my head.

<u>The Veil 'N' Fallen Rose</u>
The veil 'n' fallen rose: an abridged combustion combined
The veil
An eccentric, opaque clothe that hides the heart
Concealing the face to its abrupt society
It's worn in the street, the haven, and in His presence
Transacting in a world and in the midst of blissful people
Yet one may smile never knowing he's smiling at the veil
For it's imperceptible to its surroundings

For small laughter and modest talk may carry on
But no one can distinguish the veil
It's unseen to its public
It's a delusion and illusion to its surroundings
And you may ask what does the veil hide
It hides frustrating intuition unmentionable
It hides a warped mind in temporary custody
And still no one to cry for it but its proprietor
Yet the rose falls
Falls on what
It falls on the stone that heavy heart holds
And seems suctioned up and waxed cold
For society never fully knows
The stone that birthed the dropping rose
For this is the story abstractly told
Of the veil and fallen rose

I closed my pad and rolled the sentiments of today over
in my mind. I was in a sense hurt but more than hurt—I was
frustrated. The tears from exasperation began to roll down my
cheeks slowly. The pain inside was too much to bear and here I
was sitting on my couch crying tears of distress.

Something in the back of my mind told me that I needed
to find God. For some reason, God always seemed like the answer.
The problem was, I didn't know how to find him. I only knew a
little about him from relatives and the seldom visits to the church
but who He was and how he related to other Christians, I wasn't
aware of.

I figured in the by and by, so to speak that I would come to
know Him or Jesus. It seemed that my luck with friends and
relationships was running out. However, if I did meet God I didn't
want Him on a churchy level. This is the way that most of the
people I knew and seen had related to Him. I didn't have time for
that and besides; I was at a one shot road to fame. I didn't have
time for religious hoopla. I just figured, what's fame without good
relations? I wanted my fame to make a difference in people's lives
and without personal interaction—fame didn't mean anything. It

does no good to be famous only so that you can benefit from it. I
don't know, but I guess I'd find out.

*   *   *   *

The days passed by sort of quickly. I still hadn't heard from Tony
and only God knows where he could be. Tomorrow I had a meeting
with Mr. Johnson. I was in a way anticipating this meeting because
I knew it would be a special one. A chance at making big money
and spreading fame presented a good feeling deep inside. I had
never been at this point before in my life.

"Have you heard from Tony," Tawny asked as I clocked in.

"I haven't talked to him in days. From the sound of it, he
was talkin' out of the side of his neck."

Tawny shook her head in disgrace. "What was he talkin'
about?"

"I don't know," I shrugged. "I mean, the other night when I
talked to him he sounded like he was on somethin'." "On

somethin'," Tawny interjected. "On what?" "Knowing

him, you can never tell." I turned to go to the
dining hall.

She knew that Tony could be pretty inept at times. Heading
to the dining area I ran into Jona. "Have you seen Tony," she asked
in her motherly tone.

I dreaded to answer. "Not in a couple of days." Jona
looked at me with that "well where is he," face. I couldn't lie but
I couldn't tell the truth either. Tony was my friend and he was
probably fired.

"Tony's sick… yeah he's sick," I mustered out.

"Sick? Sick with what," Jona demanded. You couldn't just
throw out any answer to her.

"Well… he didn't really tell me; of course I didn't really
ask. But I could tell from the way he sounded, he might've had a
cold or something." I was really trying to worm my way out of it.
Jona looked like she halfway bought my lie.

"So, you couldn't ask him to see if he was alright or would
be away from work for a while or something?"

"Well, Jone, you know Tony. He could say one thing and mean somethin' else. Besides, I…"

"OK, Calvin, look if he's not going to be courteous enough to inform me then I guess his job isn't that important to him at this time. And if he keeps it up he can go somewhere else and we'll see how sick he is then." And Jona meant that.

I know at the bar and grill we would do some stupid and dumb stuff, but when it came to not taking the job serious—which almost cost me my job—Jona would cut you and she'd cut you deep. I just shrugged it off and went on about my business—it was his job on the line not mine.

I was clearing the dishes off the table from the afternoon run when heaven walked through the front door. She was the most beautiful thing I had seen. I know I've had a lot of bad luck these past few days with relationships and women but it was something about this one that made my heart freeze.

She had blackish-brown hair that flowed over her shoulders. Her pretty amber skin and black eyes gave her a glimpse of excitement dipped in the sun of radiance. She wore a red button down blouse with the sleeves just an inch below her elbows. Her stonewash denim jeans draped over her black high heel boots. She was slender framed with pretty hands and fingernails and with one hand she brushed a strand of hair out of her face and over her shoulder.

Just standing there gazing at her, she looked like Tracey Edmonds. I tried to collect myself long enough to put the rest of the dishes in the bus tub, but her beauty had me captivated. She was astonishing to the eye—a first class charm. She walked over to the bar for a drink.

Dave was standing behind the bar pretending to clean out a shot glass. "Coke please," she said in a docile tone. She reminded me of Erica except she didn't look so timid.

I sat my bus tub on the table and walked over to the counter to try my hand at conversing with her. "Hi, I'm Calvin," I extended my hand to shake hers. She looked nonchalantly at me and returned her hand for a shake.

"Listen… you looked kinda familiar so I thought I'd come

over to get your name," I lied.

"Huh, funny... I don't think I know you from anywhere," she replied. Dave sniggled.

"Yeah, well I do a lot of poetry down at the SpeakEasy Café. I see a lot of familiar faces... I just thought you were one of them." I turned and walked away feeling as if I had just made a fool of myself.

"The SpeakEasy, huh," she said as I slowed down in my tracks. "I might've seen you there a couple of times. I don't get out a lot, I work long hours sometimes."

"Oh, really? You a business lady or somethin'?"

She turned her seat towards me just a little. "Yeah, I'm the secretary down at R&G Enterprises. I do the paper work and am somewhat the brains behind the desk," she said sniggling at herself.

She had an intellectual personality and from the way she talked I knew I wasn't talking to some hoodrat or cunning seductress. "So, are you on break or somethin'," I asked trying to spark our conversation a little more.

"Yeah... I guess you could say I am. My last client I had was an early one, so I'm kinda finished for the day—at almost three thirty." She turned to the bar to pick up her glass and then turned back to me. "But, I have a few other things to do before I can technically say I'm done for the day."

Her dialect was easygoing, and she talked as one who always seemed swamped in paperwork. You could tell she didn't get out as often by her expression of the kind of work that she did. She was really an attractive and smart young woman, and I was interested in learning more about her. Hopefully I wouldn't screw this friendship up.

"Listen, I know I just met you and all, but there's a nice nightclub in town called the Black..."

"Gazon," she said, finishing my sentence. "Yeah, I've heard a lot about it... just never visited it."

I had to spark up her life—in a good way. R&G Enterprises seemed to have sucked all her interest out of life. "Well, I happen to visit that club a lot," I bragged. "I was wondering if maybe you'd like to visit it sometime? I mean… I'm sure you're a busy woman and all, but I was wondering if I could take you out sometime, as a friend of course, that's if you're not hooked up with someone else or have other…people you…could be hangin' out with."

She sniggled again at me. "Yeah… that sounds great. I'll have to see when I'm available." She moved her chair back to stand up.

"You leaving so soon," I inquired.

"I got a couple of errands to run. Maybe I'll see you around." As she walked towards the door, I could feel the independence that her character gave off.

She was leaving and I didn't even know when our "date" was or when I'd see her again. I also didn't even get her name. "Excuse me miss." She turned and looked at me as she walked out of the door. "I didn't get your name, I'd hate to call you 'hey you' next time I saw you."

She smiled slightly. "Lauren… Lauren Campton." And she walked out of Jona's without hesitation to look back. She was confident and I knew it.

I wanted to learn more about her, the question is would I ever see her again. I guess time would tell and like the saying goes: all good things come in good timing. I guess I'd have to learn that timing is everything.

11

The morning for my meeting with Mr. Dwight had arrived. I was somewhat nervous; I wanted to make a good first impression. I needed this because this would be an opportunity of a lifetime. I called Jona to let her know about the appointment and told her that I'd work the second shift to close. Jona gained a little grace after all the trouble I had been.

I ate a Pop-Tart for breakfast and had a small carton of orange juice. I couldn't eat anything heavy for the fear of it coming back up. I locked up the apartment and headed to the Camry. It was time to rock and roll.

I made it to the Starlite Coffee Shop at ten minutes to eleven. Business inside was slow and there were a couple of elderly people sitting at the bar drinking their late morning coffee. The conversation, from earshot, was of current events going on in the world.

I sat at a small table and waited for Mr. Johnson's arrival. The tabletops looked granite and were pink with a light wooden colored base. The chairs were wooden and the color of sandpaper. It was a nice coffee shop.

Mr. Johnson came in the door about five minutes to eleven. He looked like he was in a hurry or hated that he didn't make it here earlier. "Sorry I'm late... traffic."

He wore a tan suit with a white shirt and a scarlet colored tie. He was carrying that same briefcase from the other day. He plopped his briefcase down on the table and sat down. His face was slightly red from his rush to get in here and sit down. He started pulling several manila folders from his briefcase and a big black three-ringed binder. He finally collected himself.

"So, Mr. Harris, have you been thinking about what we've discussed?"

I looked intelligently at him to counteract my nervousness. "Yes... yes I have, I think a chance to really express my talent to a large company definitely sounds good."

"It's like I said, Calvin, we're always on the look out for new talent and the poetry battle coming up this Friday at the Birmingham Auditorium could be your big break."

He very well could be right. "So what will happen if I don't win the battle? Would you still consider me?"

Mr. Johnson pondered my question in his mind. I had to see if this wasn't some way for him to use me to make himself look good.

"I'll put it to you like this, Calvin, you come out and give us your all and we'll go from there." He clasped his hands together then opened the large binder. "Now, I have some of our brochures for you to look at to learn a little more about us, what we're all about... that sort of thing."

He handed me one of his brochures. I flipped it open to view the inside.

"You see, Calvin, I want you to be aware of what our company's comprised of and what we have to offer. I don't want you to agree to something that you have no idea about. That's just not good business." He opened one of the brochures and explained a little more. "Poetic Passions & Pacific is a company designed to take talented individuals and bring the best out of them whether it's by tours, promotions or what have you, we look for the best and we help bring out the best."

The information in the brochures looked well put together, and from the way Mr. Johnson talked this sounded like a good company and an excellent opportunity.

I looked at the brochure as I pondered the information over in my mind. "Yeah, well I thank you for the notification, and I'm sure I will look these materials over to see what your company has to offer."

We reviewed the brochures a little further and he elaborated on his company name, the talented poets that they worked with, their staff team and so forth. He put his folders and notebook back in his briefcase.

I was puzzled. "Is this meeting over?"

"Yeah, unless you have any more questions," he said with a smile. "My main objective for this appointment was to review our company with you and allow you time to review the brochure. Any further questions you have I'd be glad to answer."

"No, no... I just... well, I guess I just thought it would be a little more thorough," I said smiling courteously. "But I'll be in touch."

He stood up from the table. "Well, if you have any more questions here's my card."

I took the card and we shook hands. "I'll see you Friday at the battle," he said firmly gripping my hand.

When he left out of the shop I sat back down. I had the waiter to bring me a cup of coffee. Maybe the coffee would help mobilize me. As I sipped from the cup I reviewed the brochure. It basically contained a history of Poetic Passions & Pacific, a list of all the members, the founder of the company, and so forth. They were a well-established company who'd been around for 35 years. I closed the brochure and took another sip of my coffee.

I sat there and stared out the window watching the people walk back and forth down the sidewalk. Everyone walked hurriedly and carried on as if they were headed to somewhere important and exciting. However, there was one man who stood out in the crowd and caught my attention among all of the traveling people. I was stunned to the point of dropping my coffee cup on the floor.

I paid for my coffee and walked hastily out of the shop to catch up with him. He walked casually in front of me until I approached him and tapped him on the shoulder.

"Excuse me, sir," I said, as he turned around to face me. "Do I know you from somewhere?" He was the man. He was the man in the white suit with the silver-colored ponytail, the same one from my dream.

He looked at me with a slight grin. "No...sir, I don't think I do."

I paused and was evidently confounded by his presence. "I'm sorry, sir...it's just, it's just I know you...I think, from my dream."

He chuckled and made a small laugh. "From your dream? Well, that's sort of strange," he said, looking at me puzzled.

I tried to brush it off but I think I was far-gone in the fact that I had made a fool of myself. "Yeah...you told me that if I followed you you'd make me a successful man."

His demeanor changed, now showing concern with a curious interest. "A successful man you say? I, uh, well, I don't really know what to say. Success, I surely hope you find but uh... well, I'm kind of at a loss for words."

I began to get confused and somewhat frustrated. "Is this some kinda game or somethin'," I asked.

He looked at me appalled. "A game I wouldn't say, but whatever it is...it sure has you in a boggle."

I started questioning myself. Was I standing here in front of this coffee shop dreaming now? It was strange because this man's description was the identical description to the man in my dream. I had to snap out of the daze I was in and bring some closure to this.

"Are you headed somewhere, or do you have a name or card or somethin'," I asked.

He looked at me with a grin. "Joshua," he replied. I looked at him waiting for him to give me a last name or something of the sort.

"Joshua," I said, looking rather dumbfounded.

"Joshua...Jireh," he concluded. I looked at him trying to make sense of his name. On top of that, Jireh—what did that mean? Was he from another country or something?

"Joshua Jireh," I repeated. "What kind of a name is that?"

He grinned again. "Just call me J.J., hmm." He nodded and walked away not uttering another word.

I stood there trying to put the pieces together and figure out what had just happened. How was I supposed to contact him if I needed to ask him a question? He was the man in my dreams whether he admitted it or not. I hurried down the street to catch him as he got ready to turn around the corner.

"Hey," I exclaimed, chasing after him. I had to maneuver around all the people coming at me head on, busily on their way.

I continued to call out to him and scrambled to make it around the corner. When I made it around I didn't see him. There were only more people walking. I walked and walked trying to identify him but to my advantage—nothing. Well, I guess at another day and another time—I'd meet him again.

I turned and walked back in the opposite direction. I began to wonder was this man God or someone like that. I didn't believe that it was coincidental to run into a man who was the spitting image of the man in my dreams. I had to hurry back to the apartment to get ready for work.

I made it to Jona's at ten minutes to three. "Calvin, thank God you're here," Jona said relieved. "We're backed up on orders. Move down the line and help Tawny."

Tawny and I worked well together. Her mild personality and my mellow mood made our job of working together sort of easy. I liked working with her.

"What are we workin' with, Tawny," I asked.

She was preparing lettuce, tomatoes, and so forth for burger orders. "I'm getting stuff together for these hundreds of burgers we have," she said sarcastically. "You can do the onions."

There wasn't anything like a good ol' hamburger from Jona's. Here we grilled our patties to give them that flame-broiled taste. Many people who ate hamburgers at Jona's couldn't resist the taste of a flame-broiled hamburger.

I looked around and noticed that Tony was still missing.

"Tawny, still no word from Tony?"

Tawny looked at me temporally. "Naw, I haven't."

Jona passed by me and I stopped her. "Hey, Jone, you seen, Tony?"

"Uh-uh. I started to ask you where he was, but knowing him and wherever he is he's fired from working here." She kept walking showing no sign of concern.

It started slowing down about ten minutes after nine. The bulk of work now was to wash dishes, clean tables, and clean the floors. I helped clean the dining area while the others tackled the kitchen. As I wiped down a chair, Lauren came walking through the door. My heart began to flutter again.

I met her as she headed for the counter.

"Hi," she said softly.

"I guess we meet again," I replied. "What can I do for you?"

"Well, I was hoping to get something to eat before I went home."

She was so beautiful in her black button down shirt, and stonewash denim jeans. She wore her hair straight with her blond highlights showing.

"I'm sure I can help you with that," I said, snapping back to reality. "Did you wanna get it to go?"

"Sure, why not." I handed her a menu as she sat at the bar. "I'll just take a burger with fries," she said as I was preparing to give her a run down of our menu.

"OK," I said startled. "I'll get it out to you." I took the order to the back and within ten minutes her order was ready. She paid me at the counter and was out of the door and out of my presence—again.

This was twice that I let something like this happen. I couldn't pass her up on this one. I ran out the door to catch her. "Hey," I said flagging her down. I ran over to her slowly. "Did you ever check your schedule to see when you were free?"

She smiled. "Yeah… maybe we could hang out this Saturday. Maybe."

I felt the excitement rushing through my body. "But…

shouldn't you be focused on the battle this Friday," she asked.

"You know about it," I replied startled.

She smiled and turned to leave. "I get around... a little."
She turned and left and I stood there looking baffled.

"So I guess I'll see you Saturday," I said waving her off. I
thought about it, where were we suppose to meet? "Uh, where do
you wanna hang out?"

"I'll see you Friday at the battle," she replied. I caught
the hint that Friday she would let me know. She was an
incomprehensible woman—but I liked that.

I know my encounters with the women that I met would
seemingly alter my feelings and emotions, and on a more personal
level, alter my life, but for some reason this one was different. It
was something about her that projected the image of someone with
direction and confidence and that was attractive to me. Now if I
could just get my life together that would be better.

Why did I keep acting so naïve and acting as if I wasn't
up to par? Life was bigger than trying to meet women and
feeling down and out. It's like I knew what I wanted out of life
but my contradictions with self and with the people around me
sort of ruffled up confusion of mind. My run-in today with J.J.
was another strange experience. Was he God trying to tell me
something, or better yet, was God trying to tell me something? Was
this all a joke or was I in the middle of some sort of a big dream in
which I would wake up at any moment?

I went back inside and helped to close.

12

As I rode home I continued to think about my life—again. I thought about my shift of moods in poetry and how there was a contrast of "dark" and "light", so to speak. There were many insecurities that I dealt with inside. Were the women in my life the way out? Was poetry my exit? They could've been or they could not have. I ran into Lauren again tonight and she was a woman with confidence but here I was trying to work through my confidence.

The truth of the matter was that I had a dream. My dream was bigger than all the stuff that I faced on a day-to-day basis in my life. My heart was in my poetry. It was in poetry that I felt like a star among stars. The funny thing about all of this was that it wasn't until I recognized the different people that came in and out of my life that I began to see and know what and who I wanted to be.

Tony… Erica… Aliyah… Lauren, they were all mix-ups in my world. It was through my relationship and dealings with these individuals that I recognized the insecurities of an unbiased mind. What was the suppression behind it, or better yet, who was I hiding from?

I made it to my apartment around 11:50. I was somewhat tired—mentally and physically. As I plopped down on the couch, I dialed up Tony's number. The phone rang until his voicemail came on. I gave up on looking for him. If he wants to talk he knows where I am. Why did I keep calling him, I questioned myself. If he talked and acted as if he didn't have direction in his life, why bother keeping up with him.

The news and sitcoms was the only thing on T.V. and I stared at the T.V. dwelling on my doubts and sentiments until the T.V. stared back at me. I picked up my Bible and began flipping through it. I turned back to John chapter 15 where I had read earlier. I decided to read the verses prior to the earlier reading to see how this whole meaning of friendship came about as I searched in my quest for God.

I am the vine; you are the branches. If a man remains in me and I in him, he will bear much fruit; apart from me you can do nothing. If anyone does not remain in me, he is like a branch that is thrown away and withers; such branches are picked up, thrown into the fire and burned. If you remain in me and my words remain *in you, ask whatever you wish, and it will be given you. This is to my Father's glory, that you bear much fruit, showing yourselves to be my disciples.*

I closed my Bible. I had the unction to write some poetry and as I sat there with my pen and pad the rhymes poured through me and ran through my pen to the paper.

<u>Last Man Standing</u>
People come and people go
Whether they're old acquaintances or people you don't know
Different lives with different strokes
Crying together and laughing jokes
Sticking together very close
Telling secrets others don't know
With them through the sunshine
With them through the rain
With them through the good times
With them through the pain

They're there when you take flight
They see you when you're landing
But in the end, it seems, you're the last one standing

I put down my pen and pad. The next thing I remember was drifting away to sleep on the notion of uncertainty and being in Him—God that is.

I'd received a call about 6:45 the next morning. It was Juan, Tony's older brother.

"Calvin," he said, sounding alarmed. "What happened with Tony?" How did he get my number?

I was somewhat alert. "Wh… wh… what you mean?"

"Cops picked him up early this mornin'. They said him and some of his friends were caught vandalizing the city. They said he was drunk than a mutha. I don't know…"

I sat up in the bed trying to put the pieces together. "I stayed here at the apartment all night," I replied. "Matter of fact, I hadn't talked to Tony in a couple of days. I call him, he never answers. Far as I knew, I thought he had disappeared."

"Yeah, he hadn't been comin' home in the past few days. The way I figure it, he got this gal out in College Park so I figured he been out there. He may be fixin' to disappear."

"What did the cops say," I asked.

"Cops said they broke in this old rich couples home. Stole some stuff and beat the old man up for tryin' to defend his belongings."

What was Tony thinking, I asked myself "So, did they say anything else?"

"Well, they said there were some other things he and his boys may have delved into, but they ain't really sayin' much about it right now."

I shook my head. More bad news to add to the other already bad news I'd heard. How much worse could it get?

"Well, I'll let you go, Cal… thought you might knew what happened."

"OK, Juan. Listen, if you hear anything else holla at me."

"Gotcha." He hung up the phone and that was that.

It looked like another one bites the dust. If Tony couldn't hold himself up in this matter—which considering his crimes he can't—he was going to bite the dust for real.

I thought about Tony's foolishness as I cleared the dishes from the tables. As I sent the bus tray with the dirty dishes to the kitchen, my phone buzzed in my pocket.

I sat over in a booth to answer it. " Hello?"

"Calvin, how you doin', buddy?" It was Dwight. "Listen, I need to talk to you about something important." I waited in anticipation for the news.

"I got a call from the office about an hour ago about a major deal." He sounded excited and anxious all in one. "Anyway, I gotta leave out in the morning so I was calling to tell you that I won't be able to make it to the poetry bout tomorrow night. I really hate to leave you on such short notice but I gotta take this one."

Was he serious? Tell me this was just a joke? It was the day before my big break and he, my ticket to fame, had to leave out.

"Listen, ah, Mr. Johnson, is there anyway you could maybe make some arrangements to leave out Saturday morning? This poetry battle is kinda important to me."

"Yeah, I know, Calvin and I wish I could reschedule. I've tried working it out because I knew how big this was to you, but I really have to get back for this one."

And I really needed him to be at the poetry battle tomorrow night. After all the disappointments I'd experienced in the last twenty-four hours he was my last hope for a dream bigger than where I was in life.

"Well… are there any backup scouts you have that could maybe stay and cover your position?"

"Cal, you see that's the thing, I'm the only one out here representing the company but this is a major deal that has come up and I'm kinda a key player to it going through as well."

I sighed. I couldn't believe this was happening. This here was the ultimate disappointment. Why wasn't I surprised?

"Mr. Johnson, are you absolutely, positively sure there are

no other people that can represent," I pleaded. "This is my dream, my life. I can't just let it all be thrown away because you have to get back to California."

"Calvin, look buddy, I really wish there was something I could do about it, really, but I have to take them up on this one. I've tried calling around to see if there are anymore reps in the area but unfortunately I'm the only one."

I could tell he was definite in his mind. I may as well give it up. "Well, Mr. Johnson… good luck with the deal and maybe we'll meet some other time." I hung up the phone before he could respond.

I felt heavy and weighted down inside. I couldn't believe this was happening; then again—I wasn't surprised either. My life was filled with disappointments and this was just another one to throw in the barrel.

I left Jona's after four o' clock. I was bleak and aloof since my phone conversation with Dwight. I rode home thinking about all the chaos that had occurred the past few days and today.

"Jesus will be my friend… huh," I said to myself sarcastically. Where was he at? Where was God in the midst of all of this calamity? He knew this was the only hope I had left for living and here it went—up in smoke.

I continued rehearsing my conversation with Dwight over and over in my head. How in the world could this all have happened to me? I was close, so close to winning and being on the top.

I passed J.J. up standing on the corner of the street and that's when I slammed on the brakes. I put the car in reverse and backed up to where he was standing.

"Driving kinda fast there aren't we," he asked sarcastically.

I frowned and tried to brush off the blur that passed through my mind. "Yeah, just thinkin' about some things."

"You must have been thinking pretty hard," he teased again.

I once again tried to bypass the sarcasm; my life was in jeopardy, so to speak. "Look…I mean, I don't know…if you're goin' somewhere or not but um…do you need a ride?"

He looked at me with a grin. "Sure, I wouldn't mind that."

He opened the door and sat down inside. I stepped on the gas and put the Camry in the wind.

As I drove, my mind twirled in a whirlwind. I didn't really know what to ask him because for all that I knew—I really didn't know him.

"So," he started, "what's up, or what's the matter?"

I looked at him suspiciously. "What you mean?"

"I mean what's going on with you," he asked. "I see you flying down the rode and you said you were just thinking about some things, so…tell me what's on your mind."

I looked at him again skeptically. "Well, it's been a pretty shhii…crazy day," I said, being cautious of my words. "It's just… it's just that it's been one thing after the next going wrong."

"Hmm. So basically things aren't going the way you planned them to go," he said. I nodded my head in agreement.

"Look, where did you come from," I asked, diverting the conversation. "I mean, what do you do or why are you here and why were you standin' on the curb?"

He laughed out loud to himself. Apparently what I said humored him. "Why am I here," he repeated. "Well… let's just say I'm a doctor."

"Doctor," I exclaimed. "You don't look like a doctor." I looked around trying to snap back to reality. "What the heck are you even doin' in my car?"

The laughter continued. "Because, you offered me a ride."

"Yeah besides that…just out of the blue you show up. I mean I tried to find you the other time we met and poof, you disappeared in the crowd. Here I am today raising hell—in my mind—and here you are."

He gazed in my eyes as if he were looking into my soul. "Well…I sort of deal with problems," he added. "And you…well, you look like you sort of had a problem."

"So are you gonna fix my problems or somethin'," I asked abruptly.

"Well, you haven't told me what they are so how can I help." I looked at him speechlessly. I really didn't know what to say or how to tell him what was going on in my life. For some reason, and from the look on his face, I felt like he already knew

There was short period of silence as we rode along to wherever we were going.

The journey continued until he decided to speak up. "You can stop right up here at the light. I think I can manage my way from here." I stopped at the curb of a very tall building.

I looked at him puzzled. "Where you headed, man?"

"Ah, just to handle some things." He opened the car door and turned back to look at me before getting out. "When you're ready to talk…I'll be waiting to listen." He reached in his jacket pocket and pulled out a card. "Here's my card," he said handing it to me. "Call me." He then got out of the car and walked toward the corner building that looked like an executive's office.

I stared in a daze looking out of my windshield and then looked down at the card. J.J.'s Counsel Practice—what did that mean? Was he a counselor or something?

I had to get my act together and find someone else to scout me out at this poetry battle. I put the Camry in drive and moved along. At this point I wasn't sure where I was headed to but I was headed to somewhere.

13

I decided to go to the club that night. I should have been at home trying to get myself together for the poetry battle but my mind was too frustrated for that. I figured the club was the place where I could throw all of my cares to the wind. The Black Gazon was too elegant of a place, and I didn't feel up for elegance, so I found this club across town from where I stayed.

The place was full of dancers and smoke and alcohol was everywhere. What the heck was I doing here, I thought to myself. I didn't even fit in. I guess it wasn't a matter of fitting in but more like fitting out. I found a little table over in the corner where someone who looked like a waitress took my drink order. She looked like someone pulled from streets and stuck in here to wait tables. I took a club soda—I wasn't into getting drunk.

I sat there thinking to myself how my life was a mess, and I kept rehearsing my problems over and over in my mind. I knew I didn't belong in here and my conscience reminded me of that every single minute I sat there. J.J. came to mind and I still didn't know if he was God in the flesh or what, but something about him said, "morality; get your life together; or wake up and go get your dream". I thought about it and I pushed that thought to the back of my mind.

The lady brought my drink out to the table. This place reminded me of a sweltering dark cave and here I was—in a dungeon trying to cool out from my problems. I looked around trying to see if I noticed anyone in the room. I did not belong here so why in the heck did I continue to sit there; the thought kept nagging away at me. I finished my club soda and got up to leave. I knew I didn't belong and my conscience consistently kept telling me that.

As I turned from the table I heard the crowd cheering, applauding whomever it was on stage. I turned nonchalantly to see who the entertainment was when my heart almost skipped a beat. No, it couldn't be.

The lady walked off the stage and down the steps out into the crowd. I walked toward her to meet her.

"Tamica…Tamica Robbins." She looked at me surprised and utterly shocked. "You work here," I asked, almost not recognizing her. She looked so different than the last time I saw her.

"Calvin, what…what are you doin' here?" Her look implicated that she wanted me to leave her alone and go mind my own business.

I had to bring myself back to reality. "I…I don't know, I really don't know why I am here. I should be at home gettin'… my…poetry together, gosh, it's been so long since I've seen you." I was still in disbelief.

"Well, I wasn't hopin' to see you here either," she said sarcastically. "Look I gotta move around. I still got one more round to go." She walked pass me and I turned to her.

"Tamica," I called out walking toward her. "Why…why did you let yourself stoop this low?"

She looked at me offensively. "What you mean so low? I ain't low!"

I looked down at the floor trying to figure out how to reword my question. "I mean, not low, but…you were such a talented girl when me and you went out. You were into jazz… playing the saxophone…fashion model and dress. You had dreams, as a matter of fact, you use to tell me about them…what happened."

She looked at me vaguely. "Guess it was a dream…that went all up in smoke." She turned and walked away not thinking any more of it. I looked down at the floor feeling sentimental.

Here was a girl I use to date with dreams—big dreams—that she use to be excited to tell me about. She may have attracted a lot of attention when we were dating but past the drama she was just an outspoken girl with a big heart. Now here she was in a dark club dancing her life away and for what—a few dollars. The thought of it troubled me so that I left.

I got in the car and started riding. I was growing tired of the redundancy of dramatic experiences. The thought of all the relationships that I had been involved with and even the one's I messed over were tolling out on me. Tony, my use to be best friend, was now in trouble with the cops. Where was my life going? What's the use of going further if one thing led to the next?

I stopped at the park and sat there thinking. I dreamed of a better life, a life where I was a star on stage. It looked like that dream was fading away and my life felt like a box: from work to the SpeakEasy, from work to the SpeakEasy to meeting different people and gaining nothing from them. I didn't have anywhere to turn. Everything was boxing up and closing in on me.

The park was dark but so was my life. I reached in the backseat and picked up my notepad. I had to write something to get the frustration off of my mind. I turned on the light in the car and began writing.

Just Like A Dream

Just like a dream—as though it's a fantasy that's not real it seems
Like life itself it's just a hobby
A hobby with an end appearing as an illusion
Moving and transacting in a world that moves
It moves at warp speed, but it seems as if it's false evidence
Just like a dream
Life without happiness is like a sea without water Going through the motions and expecting something new But always the same result

Life—as though it seems
Just like a dream
Telling yourself, "It'll be better after a while"
But trapped in a paradise of pressure
And a weight of hurt to heavy to move
With no radiance or no gleam
As if it's a fantasy or just like a dream

It was fifteen minutes after one. I started cruising the streets again. I didn't want to go home because my mind was at work. I didn't have to go to work tomorrow so I decided that it wouldn't hurt to ride through town. I was running out of options and seemingly running out of time and life.

I sped through the streets as if my life would end in a short period of time. My cell phone rang. I looked at the caller ID but I didn't recognize the number. I ignored the call but soon after the same number called right back. Who was this playing games at this time of night? I didn't have time for games, besides—it was games that had gotten me this far.

I decided to answer just for the humor of it. "Hello?"

"Calvin," the person said, startling me as I drove. "Why are you wasting your life away?" I recognized the voice. It was J.J.

"Wasting my life away, what do you mean?"

"Have you noticed the time," he asked.

"Yeah, I've noticed—it's short," I commented. I was a man on the brink of being out of control. I felt at any moment I would burst.

"Calvin, listen to me…don't let opposition get the best of you," J.J. said.

"Get the best of me," I exclaimed. "It's too late for that. I've taken all the crap I'm gonna take. For years it has always been like this." I felt the tears flaring up in my eyes. "One frickin' thing after the next, always movin' but never going anywhere. I'm tired, so tired of it!"

"Calvin, listen to me please," J.J. said, trying to calm me down. "Life has its oppositions but it also has its opportunities. It's up to us to take the opposition and turn them into opportunity.

Now, I know you're wondering why I'm calling you at almost one thirty in the morning. I'm calling you because you wouldn't call me, even though you needed me and I'm here to help you, Calvin."

"Who are you—God?" The conversation was getting personal. I felt the animosity and rebellion setting ablaze in my heart and mind. I was tired of being a fraud to the people that I met. This was it; it was no turning back now.

"No, Calvin, not exactly. OK, my relationship with Him is personal and as one who personally represents, I try to do it well."

"So are you a preacher," I asked.

"No, Calvin, I'm not a preacher. I'm someone trying to help you."

"Well, how is it that you resemble the exact man that I had a dream about a few nights ago? The same man who told me that if I followed him I'd be successful. What's up with that, huh?" I paused and I could feel myself getting angrier by the moment. "Here I am talkin' to someone who resembles someone I dreamed about. Ugh, I must be goin' out of my frickin' mind because I know what I'm talkin' about."

There was a pause. "You ever heard of a divine encounter, Calvin?"

"What does that suppose to mean," I asked rashly.

"I'm talking about encounters where you are able to see the God in them."

"So are you a divine encounter, or whatever you're talkin' about?" My patience began to grow thin. I wanted a direct answer, not a bunch of spiritual riff-raff.

"I am somewhat divine, if you'd like to say that."

I began to get angry. "Look, who are you? Are you God or not!"

"I am your conscience, Calvin!" I became silent in somewhat of a shock. "Think about it…I'm always present when you decide to debate what's right for you or what's wrong for you. OK, the Godlike aspect of me will try to direct you to the successful and better life that is waiting for you."

I remained silent and was frustrated and relieved all in one. Here was God in the form of my conscience but the funny thing about it was that my conscience was a real person.

"I know you're wondering how can my conscience be a person," J.J. continued. "Remember…divine encounters. But let's…"

"J.J.…Joshua Jireh," I interrupted trying to put the pieces of the puzzle together.

He hesitated for a moment before answering. "Joshua… means God rescues. Jireh it means God will provide." I pondered and tried to process all that was going on.

"So what you sayin' man," I asked. "You sayin' your God who rescues and provides?"

"What I'm saying is, is that I'm here to rescue you from the so called hell you've been living through," J.J. affirmed. "I'm here to rescue you and provide you with the knowledge and encouragement you need to live out your dreams."

"What dreams," I cried. "The man who was suppose to stand witness to my gift is now on a flight back to California." The thought of it began to brood more and more in my heart. "So there it is…OK, there goes my dream."

"Calvin, listen to me," J.J. replied. "It's not the end because one man decided to go back. That's what I'm trying to tell you, it's not…" I hung up the phone. I couldn't take it anymore.

I was tired of the lies and tired of being put off and prolonged. I didn't want to hear any more. I was a man who lost all sensibility and care for any and every thing. I was out of control—and on fire inside.

14

I stopped by Milton's, a local liquor store, to buy some alcohol. I figured I could drink my disappointments away. I know it has been said that alcohol doesn't do anything but make you more depressed, but I decided to take a shot at it. I wasn't a big alcohol drinker but to hell with everything. I felt like my dream had been snatched away from me and I had to escape. The pressure was too much to bear in my mind.

When I arrived back at the apartment, I tossed the keys on the dresser. I shut my door and prepared for a late night of drunken emotion. It was going to be a long night and the party was just getting started. I'd already had enough alcohol in my system to get woozy. I had nothing to loose.

I sat on the couch and took a drink from the vodka bottle that I held in my hand. That vodka was some strong stuff. I could feel it burning as it went down my throat and by then I knew I was way in over my head. Everything was dark and suppressed, and the only thing left for me was the beginning of the end.

As I sat there out of my wits, several scriptures began to go through my head. I didn't think that the Bible would help me at a time like this—I was completely out of it. For some reason I could hear the verses in an audible voice.

"Do not let your hearts be troubled. Trust in God; trust also in me…I am the way and the truth and the life. No one comes to the Father except through me."

Where was all of this coming from? I knew that I was the only one in my apartment and surely J.J. wasn't in here. I figured maybe it was the alcohol so I got up and peeped out into the hall of the apartment to see if anyone was around. Seeing no one, I shut the door and sat back down.

"The thief comes only to steal and kill and destroy; I have come that they may have life, and have it to the full."

There it went again. I started to think that I was hallucinating… or was I. Was this God's way of talking to me, I asked myself. I thought about the dream from the other night and how J.J. told me he would make me successful.

"No eye has seen, no ear has heard, no mind has conceived what God has prepared for those who love him."

Where were all of these scriptures coming from? I had read the Bible a few times but not enough to know, or in my case, hear all of these scriptures. Some of them I had never heard before until now. What was going on?

"I am the way and the truth and the life… I am the way and the truth and the life… I am the way and the truth and the life."

I brushed it off. I staggered from the couch out onto the fire escape of my apartment as tears filled my eyes and indignation pervaded my mind. I was a drunken madman and no one could stop me. There wasn't nothing but a gulp left in the vodka bottle and I drank it and threw the bottle in the wind.

As I moved to the edge of the fire escape, I staggered repeatedly. I was out of it for real and for me it was no turning back. The plan was to toss myself overboard in hopes of escaping my pains. I was scared and determined at the same time, as I leaned over the guardrail.

"There's… nothin' left… for me now," I cried. I was scared and if God didn't send someone or something to save me I would be gone forever. As I stood there, outrageous thoughts flooded my mind.

The thought came to mind that if I jumped I'd be to others a story unread, a book unwritten, or maybe a picture yet to be painted. In the middle of my blind fury there was a hint of conscious reasoning. I figured the vodka would drown out my miseries but it didn't. It seemingly made them worse and I was caught at the crossroads of my life. I stood between two walls of decision: mindless pity or sensible discretion and for me it was a paradox, as I sat there with one leg hanging over the rail.

Jump, jump, I kept telling myself. I moved my body over a little more to pull my other leg over and now was hanging from the rail. This was it, all I had to do now was let go of the rail and it would be all over with. I kept hearing, *"I am the way and the truth and the life,"* over and over again. I tried to ignore it but the voice got louder.

Then there was, *"Do not let your hearts be troubled. Trust in God; trust also in me,"* and then, *"I am the way and the truth and the life."* The voice sounded like J.J. hanging beside me shouting in my ear. I could see his age-old face of wisdom telling me to follow him. I froze in confusion.

Let go… that's all I had to. If I could just let go of the rail all of my problems would be over with. The emotional pain became unbearable as I felt my hands slipping and my arms getting weak. Tears streamed profusely down my face as the totality of all my worries consumed my being. I couldn't face it anymore. My whole existence and way of being hung in this one moment until I heard something that diverted it all.

"Calvin… Calvin," I heard someone calling me from afar. Who was this calling me in the middle of my demise?

I heard the footsteps approaching me as the voice grew clearer. In the middle of my wretched ambition, I must have forgotten to lock the door back when I stepped in the hall. My plans were uncovered now and whoever it was would see me as I was. I had to do something.

"Calvin, oh my God, what are you doing!" I looked up to make out who it was. My face was drenched in tears.

It was Lauren. How did she get here? "Lauren, wh- wh- what are you doin' here?" The alcohol still had my speech slurred.

"Here to keep you from being stupid," she stammered. "What are you doing? Gosh, are you out of your mind?" She leaned forward to pull me up. I must have looked like a fool.

Here was a woman that I was interested in watching me, the famous poet, hang from a fire escape—how stupid. She pulled me up slowly. I could smell her perfume as she used her body strength to reel me in and once she pulled me up she sat back to catch her breath.

"Dang, as little as you are, you're still heavy," she said sniggling. "Calvin, why in the heck are you hanging from a fire escape?"

I felt foolish. "I don't know, Lauren, it's too much goin' on for me to give a care."

"To give a care," she exclaimed. "Calvin, you're a young man, you still have your whole life ahead of you. Why are you trying to waste it all away?"

"Lauren, you wouldn't understand," I stammered. "There are just some things you wouldn't understand."

"Calvin, I don't need to understand it all. OK, we all have problems but this isn't the way to fix 'em. You think if you just jump off a fire escape and end your life that'll end your problems? No, no because life will still go on with or without you, and there ain't nothin' in this world that's worth you takin' all the talent that's in you and throwin' it over a cliff."

As much as I wanted to rebuttal her, I couldn't because she was right. For some reason it was hard to put up a fight with her because her tone and demeanor somewhat sobered my ill-willed judgment. I was defenseless, plus, she was exactly right.

"How'd you find my place," I asked. "And ain't it kinda late for you to be movin' the streets?"

She looked as if her cover had been blown. "I went by Jona's earlier to look for you but I ran into Tawny. She said that you had already left for the day and I needed to talk to you about something important. So, she gave me directions to your place. I know it's kinda late but for some odd reason I felt I needed to tell you this."

I looked puzzled. "Something important to talk about, what

do you mean?" I began to wonder was this a work of J.J.

She changed postures as she began to tell me. "Well, I know this guy at work who is in to poetry and what not so he was telling me about this poetry battle tomorrow night at the Birmingham Auditorium. He told me he had to perform and that there would be some scouts from the National Poetry & Arts Association there. So I figured I'd come by to give you a heads up."

I shook my head and looked around as if reality had just come back to me. I had to get up from this misery and get myself together. Just when I thought that all of heaven had closed up and all hell had broken loose, there was a light at the end of the tunnel—a chance for me to be a star.

"So... will that be enough to get you back in the game or would you rather jump off the fire escape and end it all now," she asked sarcastically. I smiled as I stood up and shook myself. "Yeah... yeah, that should get me back on my feet." As we stood up I reached out and hugged her in appreciation.

I looked her in the eyes. "Thank you...thank you so much. You have no idea how much this means to me." Whether Lauren knew it or not she was an answer to my prayer, and she was a lifesaver—literally. She handed me the paper with the information on it and we headed for the door.

As she opened the door I couldn't help but ask. "Lauren?" I walked over to the door where she was. "If it's alright with you... you think we could still get together for a drink after the battle?"

Staring down at the floor, she sniggled at me. "Yeah... that'd be great." She turned to walk out of the door but stopped. "But no vodka." We both laughed.

She walked out of the door and I shut the door and staggered back to the couch. I guess I was beginning to sober up—I didn't see how. That vodka had me spiked out a moment ago and all of a sudden I began to think it was J.J.

As I walked back over to the couch, I sat there and started to think about what J.J. said about divine encounters. "J.J...thank you," I said, thinking on the help he offered me earlier. "I know I ain't been the best of persons to work with...but I try. I don't know if you're God or not but to you, God, and whoever else I'm suppose to be talkin' to...I'm sorry. OK, I'm sorry for all the trouble...and hell, and whatever else I put you through."

I turned and stared out of the window. "I just wanna let you know...that life, that life I read about in the Bible and the one with success that you told me about...I want it. OK, I don't want no church show, or no religious bull. I want the life...I want the life you talked to me about." I could feel the tears roll down my cheeks in my final cry out to J.J. for help.

I had nothing else to lose and no one else to turn to. All I had was a dream, and either I was going to be able to see it happen or you could stick a fork in me—because I was done.

"So whoever," I said, standing to my feet, "that I'm suppose to be talkin' to, that's from me to you." As I stood up there came a knock at my door.

I wondered who it was. I figured that Lauren may have forgotten something and she was on her way back to get it—I don't know what it could've been. "Who is it," I asked carefully. I didn't hear a reply. "Who is it," I asked again.

"It's me," someone said. I opened the door very slowly.

When I opened it there stood the reply to my prayer, or my conversation rather. It was J.J., and he was standing there in the same posture and look as he had in my dream. The feeling of deja'vu hit me all of a sudden.

"How are you doing, Calvin?"

I was startled. I really didn't know what to say. "Uh, I guess better...now."

J.J. looked at me with a smirk. "That's good to know." He looked as if he had stopped by to check on me. "That's all I wanted to know. Just trying to see if you felt better now." He turned to leave.

I had to stop him just as I did the time before. "Wait. Where are you goin'?" He turned back and looked at me grinning.

"Oh, off to the next thing," he said. "But if you follow me...I'll make you very successful."

It was just like a perfect piece to a puzzle. I wondered if my dream was a foresight to this moment. I didn't know, but whatever it was—it had me thoroughly convinced. I was assured of mind that if I followed him—and from the looks of it he seemed to be God—I would be successful.

I grabbed the notion of what he said and with that I walked back inside. I was ready for whatever and ready for life.

15

That afternoon of the next day—the day of my poetry battle that night—I sat at my desk recollecting over all that had transpired the previous days before. I began to think about Tony…Erica…Aliyah…Jona…Tamica. I sat and wondered what would become of their lives.

Tony was now about to do time in prison. Juan called me with the news earlier that morning. I felt sort of sad because he was my best friend but there wasn't anything I could do in this matter. If he did the crime he would have to do the time. I wished him well and hoped that he would find God—like I did.

I hadn't seen Erica since the day I ran into her at the mall. I figured her and Quincy were still together and getting along good. A part of me sort of felt disturbed because I didn't really get to know her like I would've liked to but it's cool. Hopefully she finds happiness with Quincy and they would do real good in life. Good was all that mattered.

I didn't know where Aliyah was. I sort of didn't wonder because of her actions and how it sort of put a damper on many things. Whatever she came to reason about her life and relationships, maybe it would straighten out her path and she could be the person she was suppose to be. I hated the conflict she caused but hopefully beneath all of the messiness there was an extraordinary person—hopefully.

I talked to Jona earlier about my poetry bout that night. She wished me good luck and said if at all possible she'd be there. I loved Jona. She may have ruffled my feathers and checked my hinges, so to speak, from time to time but over all she was an excellent mother figure. I told her of my dream to be a star in poetry and she encouraged me to go for it. I just looked at all that she taught me as a stepping-stone to where I am at this point in my life.

As far as Tamica was concerned, I hated to see how she was wasting her life away but there wasn't much I could do about it now. Maybe, like Tony, she would find God or find direction to her abandoned dreams and not waste her life away on dancing in some makeshift club.

I got up from the desk trying to shake the thoughts that flooded my mind. I had to get it together for tonight. I thought to myself of how in a short amount of time I could be well on my way across the states. No more routine or redundancy that I experienced on a daily basis. I felt free and that freedom of mind stemmed from knowing that in a moment I could be the star that I've always pictured myself as.

I walked into my room but was stopped by the ringing of my cell. It was Erica.

"Hello?"

"Hello...Calvin," she said.

"Yeah, how you doin', Erica?" I didn't know where this was going but I couldn't afford to let it ruin my focus on tonight.

"I'm good. Hey, listen...I know you're probably wondering why I'm calling you all of a sudden." She had a point. Here it was out of the blue that she decided to call me, and days prior she was with someone else. "Well, I thought about you and all the drama that's happened in the past couple of days and I just wanted to say that I know you got a big poetry gig tonight so...I wanted to wish you good luck."

That was shocking. Several days ago a kiss from someone else caused her to hate my guts and now this. "Thank you. Thank you, Erica."

"I know so much has happened between you...me... Aliyah, but I just wanted you to know that I would really like for us to just make peace and let's forget about all that has happened in the past."

"Where's all of this comin' from, Erica," I asked demandingly. "Is there a point to this or is there somethin' I'm missin'? Where's Quincy, where's Aliyah, what's up?"

"I'm not gamin' with you, Calvin. OK, I'll be honest in saying that the whole deal with you and Aliyah sort of had me shook up. Alright, she was my best friend and to think she would do something like that...ugh, I don't know."

"So let me get this straight," I began to reason. "A kiss, that totally caught me off guard, from someone you were friends with caused you to take it out on me? Erica, I'll admit that Aliyah is an attractive woman, I'll grant you that, but if I were interested in you why would I want to be chasin' her. As far as I knew, I figured Tony would be interested in her."

"You're right, you're right," Erica interjected, sounding guilty for her actions. "I should have sorted through it all and then made an accurate judgment but I didn't. OK, I'm wrong...sorry."

"Alright, Erica, hey...let's not make this a big ordeal. Let's do like you said and put the past behind us and move forward." I had to bring closure because I couldn't afford to get bogged down with emotionalism behind her. "I'm pretty sure that you and Quincy are doin' good, so...let's leave it at that."

We were silent for a moment. "You're right, Calvin," she said breaking the silence. "And like I said before...I wish you good luck."

"Thank you...Erica." I could feel the heartfelt loss and misunderstandings seeping through my phone. I decided to change subjects to subside it. "Have you heard from Aliyah," I asked.

"Yeah, a day or so ago. She is looking to get involved with real estate. Someone she knows turned her on to it and she told me that she's trying to pursue it."

That was good news to hear. Maybe now she could experience more meaningfulness in her life. She was now doing something that she found to be interesting, and I hoped that it would work out for her.

My time was short so I had to bring this conversation to an end. "Well, Erica, I gotta get myself together for tonight. If you're not busy, you should stop by and check it out." I wondered if she would come but somewhere in the back of my mind I figured she probably wouldn't.

She told me that if she wasn't too busy she might and I left it at that. We said our goodbyes and I walked in my room to get myself ready for tonight's competition.

16

This was it, the moment I'd finally been waiting for. Even though Dwight had to go back to California, I had something better—the National Poetry & Arts Association. They would probably take me a lot further than Dwight could.

I looked in the mirror as I sat there in the backstage dressing room of the Birmingham Auditorium. I had to build up confidence for tonight, and for some reason, it wasn't a struggle. I considered the entire Bible scriptures and audible voices that went through my head on yesterday's encounter. I came to the conclusion that really God must have been trying to tell me it's all about life. It's not about a religion or a church, but about a lifestyle that He created for me to have. And you know what—I think I'll take it.

There came a knock at the door. It was Lauren. "Hey," she said sweetly. "I wanted to make sure you were set for tonight."

"Yeah, I got everything I need," I replied with a voice of tranquility.

She smiled and excused herself.

"Hey," I exclaimed before she shut the door. "Listen… thank you again for everything. You have no idea how much you saved my life"

She smiled again. "Your welcome." She grabbed me by the hand. "Just do your best...OK." I nodded in agreement. She turned loose of my hand and closed the door heading out.

I smiled to myself thinking how everything had come together after so much agony and distress. I thanked God for this newfound life and thought to myself that maybe I'd be the person God wanted me to be. At this point I didn't just see Him as God— He was the God of Life. From my encounter with J.J., I learned that God also was the God of my dreams and I couldn't let him down now. I walked out of the room and towards the stage.

As I walked down the hall I bumped into Jeff. "Hey, Calvin, listen I need to talk to you," he said excitedly. "I spoke to a couple of scouts for the NP&AA. I told them how much of an inspiration you are to our café."

He grinned. "They told me if you were as good as I said you were all you had to do was prove it and they could set you up on a two year tour to do poetry on stage in different cities, promotionals over the radio—that sort of thing."

I gave Jeff a big hug. "Thanks, Jeff I owe you one."

"Just make us proud," he said teary eyed. He looked to the stage. "I think you're up now."

I walked to the stage in definite confidence. It didn't matter who or what had come into my life. This moment here... this small little inkling... this fraction of my life was all that mattered.

I grabbed the mic as I looked over the audience to see the anticipation on their faces. I noticed Lauren looking at me with support and encouragement in her eyes and I knew I had this one won.

"Tonight's piece isn't just something I made up, of course all of my poetry that I've done hasn't been made up, but it's my life experience. Throughout my whole life, it seems that I was always in search of something. For the most part I believe it may have been the success factor that I longed for. I believe we all go through life and run into challenges and circumstances, but it's the experience that makes us who we are. It's because of this experience and encounter with divinity, if you wanna call it that,

that I'm able to give you my heart, my soul, and my best.

MIRROR OF A STAR

I stood there, tears in my eyes
Pain in my veins burning like lightning in a raging rain
Animosity of the heart, distress of the soul, the huff and puff of an
inebriated break
Nothing left but my brush with death
Death? The cruelty of it makes my bones cringe
Nevertheless these are the inclinations of one who binges
Almost there
One more step and the end is near
Fire sets ablaze my eyes and body but yet engulfed with fear
Wait a minute. There it is
Could it have been a fleeting thought
An audible voice
A divine moment perhaps
An interjecting of self-realization taking abode
All is not lost, or so I thought it was
The need to press on
A soul considering in his pity
The thought of being a story unfulfilled
The reflectiveness of being a portrait unpainted
The reasoning that the time to shine is near
It is these introspects that diminish my fear
Sober my mind
Permeate my heart, all because of Divine
The realization that everyone hasn't arrived
The apprehensiveness of knowing I'm not the last
The fueling drive to go forward
Why?
Because as I look into the mirror of my life, beyond all tears
Far beyond sorrow, grief, and all fears
I say to myself in light of my purpose
I say to myself in light of my dreams
That I am the mirror of a star
You may ask what that means
When one experiences the life of infinity that is impacted by Trinity

It's as simple as knowing that everyone is a star
On stage, of life, and in all their endeavors

The audience gave me a standing ovation as they applauded and raved at a masterpiece performed. When I finished I noticed one of the scouts out beyond the crowd. I looked him in the eyes and smiled, knowing that I had that two-year tour. And from the smile and the two thumbs up—he knew I had it too.

~ With God, everyone is a star on the stage of life… and of all his or her endeavors ~

www.ingramcontent.com/pod-product-compliance
Lightning Source LLC
Chambersburg PA
CBHW070509130626
46555CB00003B/1229